# The Bloody Ripper

## T.A. Uner

This is a work of fiction. Names, characters, places, and incidents are either the product of the author's imagination or are used fictitiously. Any resemblance to actual events, places, organizations, or persons, whether living or dead, is entirely coincidental.

THE BLOODY RIPPER

Copyright © 2014 by T.A. Uner
ISBN: 978-1495289040

Cover design by Melody Simmons of eBookindiecovers
Print book design by Indie Author Services

All rights reserved. No part of this book may be reproduced in any form or by any electronic or mechanical means, including information storage and retrieval systems—except in the case of brief quotations embodied in critical articles or reviews—without permission in writing from the author.

*For Arya, more than ever*

# One

*November 10th, 1887. Victorian-Era England*

THE GREAT RED LOCOMOTIVE, *Blood*, moved with purpose through the night.

Its crew looked like any other, except for their strange red uniforms that matched the steam locomotive's exterior. The Conductor watched the stoker load more coal into the firebox. Flames leaped from it as it swallowed the coal, creating energy that drove the side rods connected to the wheels and fed the pistons, marking its impressive speed other trains could only envy.

The Conductor had been doing this for almost two hundred years, but that was before this assignment had found him. He checked the control console and it detected a railroad switch. No action was necessary as the computer would make the necessary adjustments. He appreciated the technology that Vampiress had installed. It had taken time to convince the Section Chief, but Vampiress was a woman who usually got what she wanted.

Still, it had rendered his position to one of observer status. Pretty soon his kind would be obsolete. *Does she suspect me? If so, why did she request me for this assignment?*

He didn't like The Sect, and wished he was still in the service of his previous employer, Lord Batius—now there was a vampire one could admire. But after Reptokk's armies had flushed The Sect out of Kaotika, he found his previous lord's status diminished, his position gone, the victim of Reptokk's persecution. It was unfair, but life was never fair, most of all on Kaotika.

Now here he was, on an alien world, in an era he knew little of, working as a clandestine operative with the Grand Militia. He wondered what the humans had done to deserve this? Then he remembered Vampiress and sighed.

The stoker appeared in the stairwell next to the reactor and wiped his hands on a black towel, before climbing up into the cab next to him. "*Blood* should have full power by the time we reach the anomaly," he said, knowing they had taken on much cargo before departing Liverpool Street Station.

"Thank you Rolfe," the Conductor said, "I will be grateful when this assignment is over."

"As will I, Conductor."

Rolfe's family had been taken by "The Black Arm," and offered lives of luxury and comfort in exchange for his services. The Conductor's had not been so fortunate. When Reptokk's armies had conquered Kaotika, his had been crushed under the conquering heel of the reptilian warlord's forces. Without any warning he had been forced to work for The Sect and aid them in their cause; he had travelled to multiple realities and seen many horrific acts committed by his saviors. Now his work had brought him to Earth, during its early industrial era. It seemed The Sect always chose time periods where the indigenous population could offer little resistance to Sect technology and methods.

But he was old, and longed for rest. Rolfe had been assigned here to help him manage *Blood*, it was an assignment he regretted ever since.

"I'm going to check on our cargo," the Conductor told Rolfe. "Watch the controls." The younger Vampire nodded and slid into the Conductor's seat to mind the helm.

He left the cab and passed the replica fuel bunker—filled with coal to give off the impression that this was a legitimate train of 19th-century Earth—before looking through one of the next car's windows, up at the night sky. A charcoal hue, with a smudge of a hazy full moon buried under thick wrinkled clouds. He felt *Blood* switch track under him, its process was second nature to him now. Soon they would approach the anomaly, and pass into another reality where their cargo would be delivered to The Sect.

He moved into the next car. Inside were the canisters filled with precious contents, courtesy of the Vampiress' deeds. Inside them he could see the faint glow of their contents. Some red, others were green or yellow depending on the gender or age they were taken from. The stolen items carried life-force. Through transparent tubes they were transferred into canisters where they would sleep during their voyage.

Two Black Arm operatives sat in the room, keeping a watchful eye on their ill-gotten gains. They nodded and the Conductor acknowledged them by returning the gesture. Even though it was highly unusual for him to visit this box car, the operatives did not question or suspect his motives—he was in the service of Vampiress, that was all that mattered.

"When will we reach the anomaly?" one of the operatives asked.

"Soon," he answered.

They did not question him further. The Conductor was grateful for that. He might've given himself away had they chosen to probe his mind.

He was tired of this game, it would stop, and tonight felt like the perfect time to end it. He smiled at the first operative who reached for a newspaper called *The Daily Telegraph* and began reading it. The other operative turned his back to the Conductor and started making a blood martini behind a makeshift bar. This was his chance to make his move.

He drew the silver-tipped knife from his overalls' pocket and tried remaining calm, which was not easy to do considering his precarious situation. He took a deep breath and plunged the dagger into the first operative's chest. His aim was true, slicing through the newspaper before arriving at its final destination in the Vampire's heart. The operative discharged a hiss and collapsed before his body disintegrated into dust.

Without waiting the Conductor picked up his weapon and leaped over the bar. His actions had caught the second operative by surprise, and before it could reach for its weapon, the Conductor worked fast.

His knife cut through the other vampire's wrist. It too turned to dust, but his opponent wasn't finished yet. He head-butted The Conductor, sending him sprawling backwards onto the compartment floor.

"I don't know what you plan to accomplish by this attack," the second operative said, "but you shall not live to see your plan succeed." He kicked the old Conductor in the midsection. The Conductor had taken worse blows in his long life, and had lived to tell, however, he needed to get to his feet quickly, or else his plan would fail.

The operative grabbed The Conductor by his overall straps and snarled. Despite his age the Conductor was not daunted by his task. He rammed his silver knife into the jawbone of his assailant and the Black Arm operative cursed his name just seconds before dissolving. Now he was alone. Time to finish his task. He removed the micro-disc from his pocket and stepped up to the console. He was appalled how his people had so little regard for life, even if it was foreign. Before him stood the rows of energy canisters containing the stolen lives. He overrode the computer's security program with his password, slipped the disc into the mainframe, and waited as it downloaded the information he needed to perform his task. Seconds later it fed back the information to him. With his Vampire sight and reflexes he read the instructions on how to free the trapped souls and started programming the system to release them into his disc. Seconds later his job was complete. He eyed the canisters. They no longer glowed. Empty. He slipped his disc into his overalls pocket and retrieved his knife. He would have to use it one more time, against Rolfe. Taking life was against his nature, but what The Sect was doing was more repulsive.

As he reached for the compartment door it slammed open and he staggered backwards. Before him stood four more Black Arm operatives, these were not Vampires but Hollow Men. One pointed a Gravitizer at him, but before he could act he felt his muscles freeze. "There is no escape for you, old man," said the lead operative. It was Volz, the Prefect. The Conductor stared at Volz's vacant eye sockets behind the red-tinted sunglasses.

"This is wrong," the Conductor said.

"So is betraying your own kind," Volz replied. A pulsating red hue appeared inside his sockets and spun like breaking wheels. The Conductor now saw the Prefect's sockets (where eyes should've been) highlighted by whirlpools. "Bring him closer," Volz ordered.

The Conductor felt his muscles awaken before he was manhandled by the powerful hands of the other Black Armsmen. He summoned his last bit of strength and head-butted one of them. For a moment he had caught them off-guard, and he felt their hold on him weakening. Then Volz's hands grasped his jaw and the Conductor knew his small victory would be short-lived. "Look into my eyes, old man; repent for your sins against The Sect."

The Conductor felt his remaining strength seep from within him, like a sponge being squeezed dry of fluids. "Others will rise up against your evil deeds," The Conductor said. "Our cause is strong."

"If you are referring to The Grand Militia, then you are mistaken." Volz's whirlpool eyes bore into the old Conductor's soul.

Seconds later, he felt nothing.

*November 13th, 1887. London, England*

Vampiress stared at the crowds gathered in Trafalgar Square.

The strike had started peacefully, but that was before the police had arrived. She didn't care much for this time period, or its people, but she did admit that they were passionate about their causes. Apparently this demonstration was to protest the unfair labor conditions that the working classes were forced to endure; and unemployment was also an issue here.

The Sect had chosen well. England's empire was at a crossroads, in this reality at least, and its population was ripe for the picking. There was also the matter of finding the Five who had deserted The Sect. She would enjoy hunting them down and punishing them, personally.

The police were struggling with a group of protestors when the fracas started. An English policeman was shoved in the back by a protester. He immediately retaliated by wresting a protest banner from a female protester which caused two male protestors to come to her aid.

She wanted to laugh at the primitives, fighting for basic rights that they should've had already. No wonder humans were weak, they had no unity. Her race knew how to deal with insurrections of this nature.

A group of police moved in on the rising tide of protestors, and found themselves struggling against the commoners who had armed themselves with gas pipes, knives, clubs and iron bars.

She'd seen enough and turned to leave, even though a part of her wanted to stay and watch the violence develop. It was in her nature to enjoy a good fight: whether she was involved or not, it made no difference. Casting one final look at the riot that had spread out at the foot of Nelson's Column she proceeded to her new destination, bypassing Trafalgar square fountain she found herself in Charing Cross district. A statue, cast in bronze, came into view. It was erected in honor of one of England's past monarchs, Charles I. The dedication plaque on its plinth was dated 1633.

She changed course to make her way toward Liverpool Street station. The newly-refurbished Sect locomotive, *Blood*, would be arriving within the hour, and she wanted to interview the new Conductor that had taken charge after the unfortunate incident with his predecessor whom she had distrusted enough to promote to Conductor in order to expose him as a Grand Militia agent. As always, her instincts had proven correct.

She felt a hand on her shoulder and turned around. An Englishman, a well-dressed one at that, wearing a two piece suit with a striped waistcoat smiled at her. He was stocky with a bulbous nose and his breath smelled of alcohol. "What is it?" Vampiress said crossly.

The man did not look intimidated by her defiant tone; instead, he removed his top hat and grinned sheepishly at Vampiress. "My, yer a spunky one," he said excitedly. "Juss the way I like 'em…so…how much?"

"Is there a point to this conversation?" Vampiress slipped her hand inside her cloak and gripped the hilt of her dagger sheathed behind her corset.

The chubby little man laughed. "Why of kors' there'z a point. Tell ya what, I know a quaint little hotel close by. So, I ask ye again, lass: how much?"

Of course, he probably thought she was a prostitute. If she wasn't so amused at the situation she might've been offended. She decided to play along. Vampiress opened her cloak, revealing her corseted chest and tight leather slacks. Almost immediately, the man's eyes bulged from their sockets. *That should get the old bastard's prick hard*, she thought. Across the street was a hotel. She pointed to it and the man nodded eagerly. She took his hand and led him. *Don't cum your undershorts, grandfather.* She almost laughed. When they arrived at the hotel, she pulled him into an alleyway adjacent to the hotel.

"Where are ye taking me?" he asked, breathlessly.

She smiled. "You'll see."

After walking a few meters she pushed him up against the alley wall and pressed her lips against his. She felt his hot breath mingling with hers and she felt his heart beat against her bosom. The man tried pushing her away but she kept him occupied with her kisses before she nibbled on his ear. "Dear God, yer a randy lass, aren't ye?" *Not as randy as you think, grandfather.* She moved her hand toward his crotch and felt a sticky wet patch greet her slender fingers.

"And we've only just begun," she said, casting a disappointed glance at him. "Well, I must say I'm a bit disappointed. She grasped his manhood (not an impressive size she might add) and squeezed it, hard. He yelped like a frightened puppy and tried pushing her off of him. Using her other hand she grasped his neck and found a spot. Licking her lips she sunk her fangs into the old man's skin.

He tried screaming but only a short bawl escaped his lips. He grasped her cloak's hem and tore off a small piece as he struggled to free himself from her grip. She feasted on his blood, it wasn't the best she'd tasted, but it would do, for now. After she had drank her fill she grasped his neck and twisted it around like a bottle cap. His neck snapped like a twig and she hurled his body toward the cobblestone street. His lifeless face stared up at her, pale as a sheet of typing paper. She smiled, wiped her bloody mouth with a handkerchief, and resumed her journey to Liverpool Street Station.

-+-2-+-

Today was the happiest day of Jack Mansfield's life.

He kissed his fiancé, Mercedes, and looked deeply into her golden brown eyes surrounded by a bevy of brown curls. "I'm so happy Jack," she said in her Spanish accent. He wished his parents had lived to see this day. They would've been happy to see their youngest son become a doctor. His older brother Robert poured two glasses of champagne and handed them to Jack and Mercedes.

"This sounds cliché," Robert began, "but I would like to offer a toast, to my dear brother, Jack, now a medical Doctor, and the only one of the Mansfield bothers with any sense." Everyone laughed before downing their champagne. Jack offered his hand to Robert and the two brothers shook before hugging. "I'm proud of you too Jack," Robert said. "Well done, mate." He drew a small package from the inside of his blazer. "A *small* gift."

Jack couldn't help but feel touched. This was the second gift of today. The first being a new custom-tailored suit from Mercedes. "I don't know what to say, brother," Jack said, staring at the small oblong box.

Robert smiled. "You could say thanks, and open it." Robert tore open the wrapping paper and opened the cover, inside a gold pocket watch stared back at him, on the back was inscribed: *To Doctor Jackson Mansfield, From your beloved brother, Robert*

"It's so beautiful!" Mercedes said. Taking a closer look at the watch.

"Not as beautiful as you, my dear," Robert interjected, "but a close second. Now, if you two love birds will excuse me, I must be leaving."

"So soon? Stay a bit longer brother," Jack said.

Robert put on his hat and overcoat. "Wish I could but Swanson wants to see me; it's about a new case." Jack accompanied his brother to the door and they shook hands one more time.

"Well we have some time before my family gets to London, later today," Mercedes said. "I wonder how we can spend it?" She and Jack were going to surprise them with the news that they were getting married next summer.

"I can think of one thing we can do," Jack added. He pointed to the bedroom door and Mercedes giggled.

"You *men* are all the same."

After they had made love, Jack held the sleeping Mercedes close to his chest. It was typically improper for an unmarried couple to have sex before they were joined in matrimony, but he and Mercedes considered themselves liberated from such conservative thinking. Still, her parents, staunch Catholics from Barcelona, probably would not approve of their unwed daughter going to bed with a man, even if he was her fiancé.

As she slept in his arms, he thought about how they had met at Oxford. He, the brash young Englishman from a working-class origins studying to becoming the first physician in his family, and she, the privileged daughter of a wealthy Spanish industrialist who had come to England to study English.

He thought about his future and wondered what it held. Mercedes had told him that she wanted him to come back to Spain for a few months and meet the rest of her family. He had agreed on condition that she convince her overbearing father not to interfere with their plans to live in London. He kissed his future wife on the forehead and put on a silk robe before heading to his living room. He lit a pipe and stared out the window overlooking George Street where the New Theater stood, a relatively new building, it had been built over a year ago to replace the first theater, funded by Oxford University's Dramatic Society.

He turned his thoughts back to the present. It was mid-November, 1887, summer would be here before he knew it. Soon he would be married to the most beautiful woman he had ever met. He was already a doctor, and on his way to having a rewarding life.

So why did he feel restless?

Chief Inspector Donald Sutherland Swanson was experienced law enforcement official with a sandy mustache languishing beneath matching straight hair that. A former teacher, he had decided that that career offered little in terms of advancement and had joined the Metropolitan Police force in 1868 and had risen quickly within the ranks. Inspector Robert Mansfield stood in his presence and eyed the grisly documents of the new case file that had been handed to him.

"Chief Inspector," Robert began before closing the file and taking a seat before his superior, "am I to believe that this murder victim's blood was completely drained from his body?"

Swanson nodded solemnly and took the file. "A sanitation worker stumbled across the victim's body the other day. The coroner said he'd never seen anything like it."

Robert brought the image of the fang marks into prospective and racked his brain for answers: he too had never seen a wound of this nature. "Could it of been a wild animal of some sort?" Robert asked.

Swanson shook his head resolutely. "Not unless you know of any animal that can completely drain a human body of blood. No Robert, we are dealing with a very demented killer here."

"It would take time, and a great deal of effort to siphon that much blood; and the killer would risk being detected." He glanced over the coroner's notes stating the approximate time of death. "The time of death coincides around the same time of the Trafalgar Square Riots."

Swanson nodded. "I'm putting you on the case, Robert, you're the best man I've got and I want your expertise on this."

Robert had a feeling it would come to this. "But what about the Hammersmith Case I'm on now, I'm just about to close it."

The Chief Inspector shook his head. "Bridgestone can take over for you on that." Robert didn't like leaving loose ends, especially to a rival officer like Bridgestone, who neither had his experience, or talent when dealing with sensitive cases. "I can tell you're not happy with this assignment, Inspector Mansfield, but it's very important we make headway on this case, and fast. The victim was a close friend of the Lord Mayor's, and he wants frequent updates on this one."

Robert tried his best to appear satisfied with his new assignment. "I'll get right on it, sir." He stood up and Swanson, satisfied with his response, returned to his paperwork.

The sanitation worker Robert interview reeked of alcohol and cabbage. "And you state here in the official police report that you personally stumbled upon the corpse of the victim, Sir William Denison, a prominent Banker from Uxbridge?"

The sanitation worker, a middle-aged man named Peter Hughes, had a ruddy complexion combined with a pair rheumy eyes, nodded respectfully. "Yes,

Inspector, like I said to the Bobby who took my statement: it was about four o'clock in the afternoon."

Robert nodded. It coincided with the notes in the police file he had read earlier in Swanson's office. He looked up at the sky, a dull grey, typical of London this time of year and sighed. He needed a vacation. A pigeon landed a few feet from him, bobbing its grey head as it walked and cooing. He envied the bird, it got to choose where it went and lived by its own rules.

Robert politely dismissed Hughes, who nodded subserviently and resumed his duties. Robert pulled out a magnifying glass and searched for any clues the forensic photographer might've missed (highly unlikely, but worth a look anyway). He found a small swath of cloth, unlike anything he'd seen before and he felt its fibers. It was soft, like silk, despite the fact it could be a useless coincidence, he deposited the strange cloth into his pocket. Then he headed back to Scotland Yard to show it to someone who may be able to help.

Dr. Rowan Majors was a tall, well-built Welshman with broad shoulders. He looked more like a boxer than a scientist. Educated at the Sorbonne he stood out as an expert in the relatively new field of Forensic Science. He was also a good friend of Robert. When Majors took a look at the torn cloth piece through his microscope he whistled excitedly. "Well I can confirm one thing, Robert, it's definitely, not silk. If you don't mind me asking: where did you find it?"

Robert rubbed his eyes. It had been a long day already, and he could tell already this was going to be a exhausting case. "At the scene of the crime, Majors." Despite being friends Robert always addressed Rowan by his last name. There wasn't any particular reason, but it had stuck. "I really cannot get into it now, mate. Swanson would have my hide."

"Well, I've never seen anything of this sort," Majors said. He extracted a small sample of the foreign cloth before handing the rest of the clue back to Robert who palmed it and placed it back into his jacket pocket. "Its fibers are quite advanced really. Here, let me show you." Majors led Robert into a dark room. In the corner was a strange-looking light. Majors placed his cloth sample under the light.

"This is a new technology, Robert. It's called a halogen light. Much more advanced than any incandescent light technology available today." Majors handed Robert a pair of protective goggles.

"Why are you giving me these?" Robert asked.

Majors smiled. "A precautionary measure." He flipped a switch and the experimental Halogen bulb lit up like a flare.

"Impressive," Robert said. He had never seen anything like it.

"Yes, now let's see what happens when I shine it on this piece of cloth you brought for me to examine."

Majors donned a pair of goggles and focused the halogen bulb's light directly onto the cloth sample before increasing its luminosity. Robert's eyes widened as the cloth reflected the light off of its surface.

"How can it do that?"

Majors dimmed the light and removed his goggles. "When I find out you'll be the first to know, Inspector."

Jack couldn't help but laugh at the fortune teller.

"Well of course she's going to meet a mysterious man," he told the old woman, who was doubling as the pub's barkeep, "It's me."

The other patrons around Jack and Mercedes laughed so hard; one man nearly gagged on his pint. "All in a night's work, my loves," the old woman said, her name was Molly and she was quite popular with all of the customers at the *Sword & Lion*, the pub he frequented in Piccadilly Circus. Mercedes had been hesitant at first, but she had warmed to the place since Molly the barkeep always made everyone feel welcome.

"Where is Robert?" Jack looked at his new pocket watch. It glimmered under the pub's smoky lights.

"He'll be along shortly," Mercedes said reassuringly before planting a warm kiss on his cheek. Her breath smelled of mint, he always wondered how she kept it smelling so fresh, even when she drank alcohol.

A few drunk patrons in the corner began singing a cheery tune. The warmth of the song did little to calm Jack, who always worried about his older brother: perhaps it was because of Robert's dangerous line of work.

"Maybe the Vampire woman got him," said a portly man sitting next to him. He had a square nose and wore a drab brown suit. The shadow from the brim of his derby concealed his eyes.

Molly looked at the man and hissed like a balloon. "Now Seamus, don't you be spewing that rubbish again. Everyone knows it's all a bunch of shit."

Seamus shook his head and removed his derby, revealing a bald head dotted with freckles and two sharp eyes positioned under bushy brows that made the man resemble a fox. "It's true, and anyone who doubts me can read about that dead banker from Uxbridge in *The London Bugle*."

"Don't listen to him, Jack," Molly said as she polished a tankard. "He's one of those folks who reads those new tabloid papers that everyone is now into. If you ask me, it's all just a passing fad, really."

"Ignore me at your own peril, young doctor," Seamus said. Molly snorted her disdain and turned to greet a new patron that had stepped up to the bar.

"I'd like to hear more," Jack said. He figured he'd kill some time while he and Mercedes waited for Robert to arrive. Seamus nodded and hopped over to the next stool to get closer to Jack and Mercedes.

"A wise choice," he said in a thick Irish accent, extending his hand. "Seamus McCoy, Private Investigator." Jack shook his hand. Despite being a diminutive fellow, Seamus had a strong grip, and the skin on his fingers were coarse.

Jack introduced himself and Mercedes, who smiled politely at the private investigator before returning to her drink.

"Without violating any confidentiality agreements," Seamus said sheepishly, "I can tell you that one of my past clients hired me to investigate a strange occurrence up in St. Albans, Hertfordshire; one of his accountants had disappeared, naturally he cared about all his employees, so he hired me to find him." Seamus paused to take a sip of his drink while Jack waited patiently for the Irishman to continue the story. "It was near the railway station."

"What *was* near the railway station?" Jack felt his shirt collar stiffen, while his pulse quickened.

"The employee's body; it was drained of blood."

"That's preposterous!" Mercedes said. Jack placed an arm on her sleeve and motioned for her to calm down, apparently the alcohol had lowered her inhibitions.

"It's true, lass…Vampires are out and about in the country. For what reason only God knows."

"Amazing how I've never heard of anything of this sort before," Jack said.

Seamus coughed into his fist. "And risk a nationwide panic? I think not, Doctor. No, these bloodsucking monsters are here for a reason."

Jack did not know why, but he believed Seamus. The serious look on the Irishman's face was all he needed to be convinced. Besides, he did not look like the type that lied. Call it a hunch. "Well it's been good talking to you and your lady friend, doctor, be safe." He downed the rest of his beer before placing a few shillings next to his empty beer glass. He tipped his hat to Jack and Mercedes and sauntered off.

"You didn't believe any of that foolery? Did you beloved?" Mercedes asked. "He's obviously drunk, a liar—and a bad one at that."

As Seamus left though the pub's doorway, Robert appeared. "There he is," Jack said standing to greet his brother. Mercedes kissed Robert on the cheek and Molly brought over a bottle of Irish whiskey.

"Sorry I'm late Jack; new case I'm working on." Jack asked for a table so they could be more comfortable. After they were seated Jack watched his older brother drink his whiskey in silence.

"Is everything alright, Robert?" Mercedes asked, placing her hand on his arm. Robert not being one to shun female attention, especially from his future sister-in-law squeezed her hand appreciatively.

"Thanks for asking, my dear; it *has* been a long day."

Jack ordered some lamb and potatoes for his brother. "Some food will do you good, Doctor's orders, mate." Robert smiled curtly. *Very unconventional behavior,* Jack thought. *Even for one as professional as Robert.* "Can you talk about it?" One of the waitresses brought a steaming plate of food and Robert tucked in.

"It *is* a strange one at that."

"You should've been here a few minutes ago," Mercedes chimed in. She had ordered another drink and Jack hoped his distinguished fiancé would not become too inhibited as the night wore on. "There was the strangest man sitting next to us. *Tell him,* Jack!" She playfully prodded jack with her fingers. He squeezed her hand in reciprocation, as if to warn her of becoming too excited.

"It's true," Jack began, "strange bloke he was, an Irishman."

"I'm sure our neighbors to the north find us English a bit odd as well, brother," Robert replied coyly.

"No this is something about Vampire creatures, Robert. Apparently this Irishman found one if its victims—the corpse was completely drained of blood."

At the mention of Vampires, Robert stopped eating and grunted.

"What's wrong, brother?"

Robert wiped his mouth with a napkin and took a deep pull of his lager. "There might be some truth to what that Irishman told you."

"Explain." Jack leaned in closer. *I wish you would tell me what is bothering you, brother.*

Robert lowered his voice and leaned in towards Jack. It didn't make sense, all this secrecy, not like anyone was listening, and if they could the noise from the pub would easily drown out their words. "I can't get into details, but I'm currently on a case that shares eerie similarities with what you've just told me."

There was a loud crash. Both Jack and Robert turned around. One of the bar patrons, an obese man wearing a tight vest over his large belly had fallen over a table, or what was left of it.

"Tell me more," Jack said.

Robert looked around to make sure no one was listening. "The only thing I can say is…be careful."

# Two

"This time you've gone too far, Vampiress!"

Her Section chief, a Vampire called Ambrogio, was fuming. Hardly surprising. The man was as volatile as an explosive device. It amazed her how fast he had risen up the within The Sect Hierarchy. He stood up from his leather chair and began pacing in front of an elaborate bookcase. "Do you know the man you killed was a close personal friend of the Lord Mayor of London?" At the door two Hollow Men stood at attention. They watched her with their indifferent expressions. Beneath their sunglasses she could see the whirlpools that made up their eyes. If you could call them eyes.

"I don't make it a priority to learn the names of my victims. Really, Chief Master, to me there isn't much difference between these inferior humans. They're all look like food to me. I just had a snack that's all."

Ambrogio walked up to her and stopped less than an inch from her face. She could smell his hair tonic. She felt like shooting an arrow through his chest. Then she repressed the urge. *Probably not a good idea with two Hollow Men in the room.* "That has always been your problem, Vampiress, you don't make anything a priority! Your reckless behavior could've cost us this mission. If your father wasn't good friends with the Viceroy I'd sack you myself."

She knew that he meant it. But then where would he find a suitable replacement to fill her position? Few possessed her skills and experience, and despite her father's lucrative connections, she felt it was unfair for Ambrogio to imply she wasn't qualified for this mission.

"But you won't," she snapped. "We both know how important this mission is."

He shooed her words away as if they were gnats and reseated himself. "You know of the insurrection on *Blood?* The Master Conductor was caught trying to liberate the canisters' contents."

"Yes, I read the report."

The Chief nodded, then, eyed his tablet. "Good. I want you to go to the rail station and interview the new Conductor, Lok. I want to make sure that he understands his role. If not I cannot have another rebellion when we are so close to victory in this reality."

"But I've already interview Lok. He checks out. No suspected connections to the Grand Militia." *You pompous arse.*

"Then interview him again—dismissed!"

She returned to her personal quarters downstairs and threw herself into her chair. Outside the sunlight passed through her window but the shield generator in the basement protected all the Vampires with the sunlight filtering field. No harm could come to them. The Hollow Men were safe regardless; nothing could kill them, except silver.

She opened her closet and checked the supplies before taking out her quiver filled with her arrows. She chose one arrow, with a silver-tipped head, and started inscribing Ambrogio's name on it.

─ 2 ─

*August 31st, 1888 Buck's Row, London, 3:50 a.m.*

Dr. Rees Ralph Llewellyn looked at the body of the dead woman lying on the sidewalk and pronounced her dead. "I'll have to run a full autopsy of course," he told the two Police Constables who had summoned him to the murder scene, PCs Neal and Thain.

Thain started taking down notes on a pad while Neal went to fetch an ambulance to haul the body down to the coroner's office. When Robert saw the autopsy pictures of the dead prostitute, one Mary Ann Nichols, he couldn't help but recall the case he had worked on last November. Swanson had gotten on him back then when he had worked on the case, the lack of evidence was frustrating, and despite making headway the case was ruled inconclusive, and thus declared unsolvable.

It was a giant slap in the face for Robert Mansfield, the impressive Inspector, who had solved many high-profile cases in the past.

Now, here he was, almost a year later. Working on a similar crime. This time the victim was a woman, and a prostitute at that.

"You'll be working directly with me on this one, Mansfield. And this time no muck ups. The last thing London needs is a general panic about a deranged serial killer prowling the East End."

Robert didn't like being associated with the words 'muck ups.' He was determined to make positive headway on this case. He owed it not only to the victim, but to his own sense of professionalism as well. He knew Swanson was under a great deal of strain, having been appointed by Robert Anderson, Assistant Crime Commissioner, to head this case, but Robert wanted to crack this case badly, more than any other he could recall.

"Go interview the deceased's spouse. He's down at the coroner's office now," Swanson said before returning to his never-ending paperwork. Robert did not envy his superior's position.

Down at the coroner's office he found William Nichols. He was looking over the remains of his former wife. A dour look plastered across his careworn face.

"Mr. Nichols?"

Nichols turned toward him. "Yes?"

Robert offered his hand to the widower who looked at it indifferently before shaking it. Nichols' hand felt cold and clammy like a dead fish. "I'm Inspector Mansfield, I've been assigned to this case, may I speak to you for a moment?"

Nichols nodded.

"When was the last time you saw your wife?"

Nichols paused for a moment, as if trying to understand the question posed to him. "Three years, and yes, I knew she was working as a prostitute."

"I see." Robert took out his notepad and started scribbling down words.

"She deserted me, and the children, you know. And when I learned she had become a woman of ill-repute, I discontinued support payments to her."

"What else can you tell me?"

"Nothing, may I go now Inspector?"

"One more thing, Mr. Nichols, does your former wife have any living relatives?"

Nichols nodded and gave Robert an address for the residence of Edward Walker, her father, living in Camberwell.

Robert journeyed to South London and found Mary Ann Nichols' father. Edward Nichols, a wide-shouldered man who worked as a Blacksmith, greeted him cordially at the door and told Robert how dissolute his daughter had been during the time she had lived with him. He claimed she lived in various workhouses and was a habitual alcoholic whom he knew would come to a bad end. Robert took copious notes, thanked Edwards and left.

As he was leaving he passed by Honey Mew's near Brady street he heard a woman calling out to him from a doorway. As he approached her she looked around cautiously, to check if they were being watched.

"I know about the Nichols murder," the woman said.

"Bad news travels fast," Robert replied, "and you are?"

She looked around again before answering, "Mrs. Sarah Colwell." Robert read fear in her eyes, the murder had to have ruffled the residents of this neighborhood, Robert thought. "Are you with the press?"

"No, Scotland Yard." He showed her his badge. She cast a frightened glare at him. "Come inside Inspector," she said, hurriedly trying to usher him into her home. "We can talk more comfortably in my home."

Robert looked around the modest home. It was well kept. Colwell brought him a cup of tea and he thanked her. "Now, what can you tell me of the murder, Mrs. Colwell?"

Mrs. Colwell took a sip of her tea and paused for a moment, as if collecting her thoughts, which reminded Robert of Nichols' husband. *They both want to make sure they give clear depositions.*

"It happened last night," she began.

Robert's eyes narrowed. "*What* happened exactly, Mrs. Colwell?"

She leaned in closer to him; her blue eyes fixated on him. "I heard a woman yelling 'murder, police!'"

Robert started scribbling notes. "At around what time did you hear this?"

"I'd say a little after midnight, at least that's what I told the press, all the major papers, and some of the local ones." Robert tried to conceal his disappointment. *Then it would be only a matter of hours before the details of this murder are everywhere.* He pressed on. "What else can you tell me about this woman who was yelling?"

"Not much. Did you find any other witnesses? Maybe she came forward."

"No one has come forward yet, Mrs. Colwell."

He asked her a few more rudimentary questions, and, when realizing that she indeed had no more to offer, excused himself and hurried back to his office to file a report.

He hated writing reports.

― 3 ―

*September 4th, 1888*

After breakfast Jack took his paper and unfolded it. He had been married for a few short months, since June, and had spent the next two months traveling Spain. Now he and Mercedes were back and he was anxious to begin his residency training as a physician. He had read through the various stories and had had enough indoor activity. Just as he put the paper on the coffee table he noticed the headline. It read: **Leather Apron Murderer on the loose. Scotland Yard baffled.**

He felt his heart pause for a second before it resumed beating. Then he started reading the article. It went into detail about the recent murder in Buck's Row of a woman named Mary Ann "Polly" Nichols by a mysterious assailant. What caught his attention was the mention of Chief Inspector Swanson, and his brother Robert being named as the main police investigators assigned to the case. A part of him felt for his brother and he wished that his name had been spared in the papers. But that was the life of a policeman.

Mercedes was out shopping and would later be at her ballet lessons so he put the paper away and went for a walk. It was warm for September and the sun was at its zenith, and, except for the occasional cloud the sky was clear. Jack started walking faster, the article had given him a bout of anxiety and he wanted to work it off with a good walk. A sweat broke on his forehead and he felt better. He found a café on Oxford Street and ordered a cup of tea.

As he sat outside sipping his tea, Jack couldn't help noticing a woman walking on the sidewalk near his table. What made her stand out was the black cloak she wore. He thought it a bit strange considering the warm weather and was about to return to his tea when he noticed something that made the woman's presence more outlandish.

Around her he could see pedestrians casting long shadows under the fretful sun rays, but this woman...*she had no shadow.* At first he thought his eyes were deceiving him. He squinted as he followed her motions. *Still no shadow.* He dug into his pocket and deposited a few coins next to his tea saucer. She was getting ready to cross at Oxford Circus, Oxford street's busiest intersection. He would lose her if he did not act fast. So he ran.

To Jack's credit he did not lose her. He had fought in the first Anglo-Boer War in 1880, and despite suffering a leg wound at Transvaal, he had been able to fully recover, so this burst of speed did not impair his gait.

He almost lost her in the crowd. But managed to catch her entering a blacksmith's shop. He waited at a safe distance so she wouldn't spot him (she struck him as a woman who was alert) and when she emerged from the shop he though he saw a bulge on her back, underneath her cloak. She turned around for a moment to look about and adjust her corset before continuing. Her long black hair flowed over the back of her cloak and if it wasn't for the brightness of the sunlight it could've easily blended with the cloak.

He walked for close to an hour. No. He was not mistaken. She still had no shadow. It was amazing that no one else noticed it. When she arrived at Kingsbridge, she disappeared inside Harrods's. This time he decided to follow her inside, certainly there would be enough human presence inside to allow him cover.

Inside he watched as she walked by various outfits and inspected them. Once inside the building he noticed how pale her skin was. Almost as if her skin was made of paste. It did not distract from her looks though, she had a long curved nose that blended well with her brimming lips and statuesque cheekbones. She turned and looked around again. He saw a display of neckties and acted like he was browsing for one.

A sales clerk approached and greeted him before asking Jack if he needed any help, but he politely declined. By then, the mysterious woman with pasty skin had disappeared from her previous spot. *Damn!* He ran from his spot, leaving the surprised clerk in his wake, just in time to see her passing through a revolving door. He stopped until she had cleared it before following.

Outside he turned to his right and saw her ducking into an alley. The cloak billowing up behind her, he saw a quiver strung to her back and she wore tight leather slacks over black studded boots.

Jack continued his relentless pursuit. He saw her turn right and duck into another passageway. When he reached that spot, she was gone. He looked around. No sign of her. He cursed but made a mental note of this location and started back towards Harrods when he heard the sound of various trash cans being knocked over. He turned around quickly and saw a glint of light speeding toward him. He ducked sideways just as the blade swished by his arm, catching the sleeve of his jacket. The weapon tore through it and he felt the hot sting of blood. He pulled a handkerchief and pressed it against the wound, which was not serious, before tying it around his arm. He had gotten off easy with a flesh wound. It could've easily pierced a vital organ had he not been nimble.

He walked towards the spot where the knife lay and picked it up. Even on a balmy day like today the hilt felt cold in his palm.

He looked at the blade. There were strange runes inscribed in it. He held it up to the light and still could not make anything of them. Upon further inspection he noticed an insignia inscribed on one side of the hilt. It resembled a coat of arms where a red-eyed bat with outstretched wings stood on a crest depicting two crossed swords. Wrapping the knife in another handkerchief, he slipped it into his trouser pocket. Jack decided he'd seek help of an expert before going to the police. After wracking his brain for the Irishman's name he finally managed to recall it.

But first he would need to find him.

It took him a day but Jack was able to track down the office of Seamus McCoy.

Having an Inspector for a brother helped, and he traced McCoy's office to London's Southwark district. He took the tube and arrived late morning. The office was on the first floor of an elaborate building designed in Georgian architectural style. Jack knocked on the door to the office and was greeted by McCoy himself. At first the Irishman squinted as he tried to recognize his visitor. Then slowly, a polite smile formed on his lips. "Why Doctor, to what do I owe the pleasure of your visit?"

"May I come in, please?"

McCoy opened the door and waved him in. "But of course, Doctor, come in, come in," he said joyfully. McCoy offered Jack a cup of coffee but he politely declined.

The office was not very big; two bookcases filled with tomes lined one wall of the office, while an oak desk stood in front of a lone window. Jack was anxious to show McCoy the knife that had been hurled at him. The Irishman looked over the wrapped knife with relish. "What is this, Doctor?"

"I was hoping you could help me answer that Seamus." McCoy took a seat behind his desk and donned a small pair of half moon spectacles.

"Quite an interesting weapon, Doctor. Might I ask how you obtained it?"

"Someone tried killing me with it."

McCoy's left eyebrow rose. "Indeed. Care to tell me more?"

Jack told McCoy his story of spotting the shadowless woman with pasty skin on Oxford Street who was overdressed for a balmy day, and how he had tracked her to Knightsbridge. "I remembered our discussion at *The Sword & Lion* and decided to come find you."

McCoy nodded and continued inspecting the blade. He pulled out a magnifying glass and took a closer look at the Bat roundel on the knife's hilt.

"Have you ever seen a marking of that kind?" Jack asked.

"Good question, doctor." McCoy looked up and pulled a thick tome from the bookshelf. Robert waited as the Irishman flipped through pages and mumbled to himself. "I think I may have something, it's only a lead but for right now it's all we have to work with." McCoy pushed the book toward Jack and pointed at a logo printed on the book's page. Jack noticed a bat-like creature printed on the page, underneath it, the caption read: Vampire Bat.

"So it is true," Jack said. "Vampires *do* exist." McCoy smiled. "Well, of course they do, Doctor. I thought we had agreed on that subject the other night."

Robert didn't want to tell McCoy that he was only trying to be polite the other night, especially in front of Mercedes. But now the evidence was clear.

"One fact that eludes me is, how this female vampire was able to stay alive during the day. Vampires are nocturnal creatures by habit and sunlight is capable of destroying them." He took the knife again and carefully ran a finger down the blade's fuller. "I'm no expert in metallurgy, but I have a feeling this is no ordinary metal found today, even with all the technological advancements."

Jack thought about how automobiles had become popular in the past few years. The days of the horse-and-carriage were numbered. "So can you help me?"- Jack said.

"Depends on how you define '*help*,' doctor. Do you want me to investigate this vampire woman? Or simply give you advice on how to proceed?"

"Both." Jack owed it to himself to track down the person who wanted to kill him, perhaps it would shed light on some unanswered questions. "I will pay you of course Seamus."

McCoy smiled. "If I take this case it wouldn't be for money, doctor. You made the right decision by coming to see me for advice, and, I am quite intrigued by the case."

"So when can we start?"

"Can I hang onto this blade for the time being?" Seamus asked. Jack nodded; Seamus wrapped the knife and put it in his top desk drawer before taking his hat and jacket off the coat rack. "We can begin now if you like?"

They took a taxi back to the spot where Jack had last seen the woman. AfterMcCoy had been satisfied that no clues existed they walked to Hyde park to discuss their next move.

"Why do you think Vampires are here?"

McCoy lit a cigarette and they found a park bench to sit on. "They obviously have an agenda. It could be anything from harvest human blood to manipulating our social development. Or maybe something completely different." A group of pigeons gathered in front of them and started cooing.

"Such as?"

McCoy inhaled deeply from his cigarette and exhaled smoke. The pigeons obviously didn't agree with the fumes, they scattered like frightened children. "There have been rumors of a strange red locomotive coming and going from Liverpool Street rail station. The police boarded this train on two different occasions, but found nothing, except empty canisters."

"That doesn't say much," Jack answered irritably.

"No it doesn't, except that one day I went to investigate and noticed that when the canisters were being loaded, some of them glowed. It's as if they were transporting some sort of energy." This still didn't amount to anything in Jack's mind. He actually felt more confused than before he had come to ask McCoy for help. McCoy picked up on this and patted Jack on the leg. "But we'll find out what these blood-sucking fiends are up to doctor, I've been a private investigator for over ten years, and there is nothing I dislike more than not having answers to the questions I seek."

Vampiress' attendants undressed her before she lowered herself into her bath. They poured warm water and cleansing oils into the tub and soon she felt her body relax. The filth of this city never ceased to amaze her. Even when her people had been at war with Reptokk's forces, the upkeep was always excellent in all their major cities. She was eager to forget the past few days. First, the argument with the Chief and yesterday's cat-and-mouse game with the well-dressed Englishman. *Why was he following me? Does he know why we're here?* As she racked her brain for answers her attendants scrubbed her arms and back with soft brushes. The soft follicles felt good on her skin as they cleansed her of London's grime. She would be glad when her assignment here was over.

Vampiress turned her attention back to the Englishman. There was no technology available in 19th-century England that could track her. In this timeline the invention of crude radar technology was still decades away; GPS technology, a century away. They had no scanners, or dispersal fields capable of penetrating Sect cloaks. Yet this man had found something that pointed her out to him. Of course. How could she of been so careless. After ordering her attendants to leave she checked her service belt. Her fears had been confirmed. *How could I be so fucking stupid?* she chided herself. *A senior field operative making a mistake a first year Plebe wouldn't commit.* She had forgotten to engage her shadow enhancer. No wonder the human had been able to find her. She was lucky more humans had not noticed she lacked a shadow. Vampires were considered fables in this time period. However unlikely, this human apparently had some sort of training, or knowledge about her kind, otherwise he would've never been suspicious enough to follow her.

To much was at stake for a careless mistake to undo all of her hard work. It was required protocol to report this to her section Chief, but that would only cast more doubt on her. She knew he had little love for her aristocratic blood. Besides she didn't want to give the old fool an excuse to dismiss her. Then she would be sent back in disgrace.

The Sect had already suffered a setback in another reality. Two Hollow Men sent to 2146 Florida on Earth had failed to incite a Zombie assault which would've won them an important victory, and secured that timeline for The Sect. The evidence retrieved from their emergency recorder beacon indicated their mission had been foiled by a Cyborg and a mutant reptile called a *Crocodile*. The last thing Vampiress wanted was another failed mission, especially one where she had been given full command over field operations.

Her attendants returned to dress her in a Victorian outfit. After dismissing them again she re-armed herself with a small havoc pistol, a less obtrusive Sect weapon, (she hated leaving her bow and quiver behind, as this was her weapon of choice) and headed for Liverpool Street rail station. This time making sure her service belt countermeasures were activated.

"We're behind schedule, and the Section Chief is not pleased."

The new Master Conductor, Lok, looked at Vampiress abashedly. She could tell that he and the stoker, Rolfe, had little affinity for her. "I am sorry mistress," Lok said politely. "We've been experiencing issues with some of the transport fail-safes that monitor the canisters. My technicians are currently repairing it; rest assured, the problem shall be corrected before our next scheduled departure."

Vampiress knew it would be premature to micromanage the new Master Conductor, he had only just been promoted to his new position aboard *Blood* and had inherited the unenviable task of cleaning up the mess left by his predecessor. The insurrection had caused much distress within Sect headquarters. As a precautionary measure, the entire staff of the previous crew had been executed, except for Rolfe, who had somehow managed to convince the Hollow Men of his innocence.

But the Hollow Men crew of the previous crew remained. To punish them would admit that The Black Arm, the Sect's secret police were at fault. The Hollow men were their proudest accomplishment. With the exception of the failed Florida mission their reputation was pristine. But she didn't come here to inspect the locomotive, that was just a cover for her true purpose.

"Then carry on." The Master Conductor and his stoker bowed their heads respectfully at Vampiress and returned to their work. She left the first box car and worked her way to the end car, or caboose as the humans called it.

When she opened the door she was greeted by a Hollow Man. He looked at her with its blank expression. *Neither Vampire, nor Machine, yet both,* she thought.

"State your purpose," it said.

She hated the way they showed no respect to her rank. She was a Senior-level field operative. "I need access to the Sect master computer," she replied curtly. Not pleased that she had to explain her actions to this creature.

Vampiress could see the whirlpools behind its red sunglasses. For someone who had undertaken dangerous missions, and fought against impressive adversaries, those whirlpools still made her uneasy. "For what purpose?"

She felt like pulling out her havoc pistol and vaporizing this being. But that would put her at dangerous odds with Sect Command. "I'm on official business, and I do not have time to sit here and discuss operations. Now, let me pass."

"I must have confirmation," it said. The whirlpools beneath its sunglasses increased in celerity.

"Do you want me to contact the Section Chief and tell him you are delaying official Sect business?" She waited as it digested her words.

"No, that will not be necessary, Vampiress," it said, stepping aside. She pushed her way past it and sat behind the blinking console. Before she started her work she turned around. The Hollow Man was still standing there in his black suit and tie with red dress shirt.

"I require privacy for my work," she said. When it did not respond she raised her voice: "Get out." It turned around and left the end car.

Fucking freak. Her fingers danced across the console, trying to obtain the information she sought. With her security codes she had been able to access the surveillance drones that kept watch over London. Hidden by their cloaks they were undetectable. She accessed the time index she was looking for and located the image of the man who had followed her relentlessly yesterday. She magnified the image and took a closer look at his face. For a moment she felt her past collide with her present, the imaging sensor told her this man's face matched the records of one Jackson Mansfield. But it reminded her of Renault, and that cursed day, many years ago, before Reptokk had driven her people from their homelands.

Before she had became a temporal assassin for The Sect, she was an unassuming young girl named Fiolia, living in the Capitol city. This was years before her people had gone to war with Reptokk's armies.

One afternoon, her father had taken her and her twin brother, Renault, outside the Capitol for their first hunt. They climbed atop their Bloodbat, Riser, an armored flying bat that were bred specifically for aerial duties, and headed for the red mountains. Uk-rett, which meant "Black Sun" in Kaotikan, its silhouette simmered in its perpetual state of eclipse within Kaotika's crimson sky. Fiolia had always wondered how a star could still shine despite being obscured by another planetary body, her tutor had once explained the phenomenon to her during one of her astronomy lessons, but she could not recall what he had said.

She heard a loud sound that sounded like an explosion and gripped Riser's saddle. "It's only a patrol craft," her father had said reassuringly.

That still didn't reassure her. It had Maratak markings, and they were a race of Demons that shared a border with her people. An uneasy truce existed between The Sect and the Maratak Confederacy. But that meant nothing in Kaotika, the Maratak were a capricious race with a warlike nature. She remembered how Renault had once explained to her how the Maratak had once been the dominant species on Kaotika long ago, during their expansionist era, when they had built a space empire from the hundreds of star systems they had conquered with their space fleets.

"It's an Intruder-class fighter craft," Renault said. The vessel picked up speed and headed back toward Maratak territory.

"What if it comes back?" Fiolia asked.

"Don't be stupid," Renault said. "They're still recovering from their war with the Vastars, they wouldn't dare go to war with us during their reconstruction."

"Renault, don't call your sister names," their father said before steering *Riser* over a forest. Below them Fiolia could see a land bridge stretched over a major river that snaked through a gully.

"The Eternal River," Fiolia said in awe.

"Why is it called that, father?" Renault asked.

"Legend claims the Kaotikan Gods created it to mirror their immortality. It has also been used to transport goods throughout the land." *Riser* began his descent. They passed through a thin mist and for a moment Fiolia could not see around her. It quickly filtered away and they landed in the middle of a large clearing where a careworn path disappeared into a lush rainforest.

"Make sure you get your supplies, children." Fiolia hated it when her father addressed her like a child. She suspected that Renault felt the same way, but the boy would never admit it to their father. After they had set up camp she watched her father whisper words into *Riser*'s ear. The Bloodbat reared its head and took off. Its leathery black wings carrying it up toward the sky.

"Why did you send *Riser* away?" Fiolia felt safe with the great creature around. "Shouldn't he stay and protect us?"

"My girl, you must learn to rely on yourself. You cannot always count on others for protection. That is why we are here. To help improve both of your survival skills."

She didn't want to be here and didn't understand why her father placed so much importance on this trip. Their family was firmly entrenched in the upper echelons of Vampire society, her father was a baron and a valued member of the Capitol's ruling council.

"What's for dinner?" Renault asked.

"Get your bows," her father told them, "we'll be catching our dinner tonight."

They left the campsite and as soon as they entered the forest the light faded. Only a few stray thin rays filtered through the treetop branches. "It's dark in here."

"That is the purpose of the hunting exercise," her father said. "If we were to carry a lantern it would frighten game away." They climbed over a fallen tree and the baron led them into a dense patch of foliage.

"What are we doing in these bushes?" Renault asked.

"Quiet!" the baron said in a hushed voice. "You mustn't talk. We're on a hunt, not a leisurely walk through the woods." They moved about the foliage, careful not to attract attention. Their father soon pointed out a target and ordered Renault to shoot it. It was a green pheasant, known for its tender, juicy meat. Her stomach rumbled, Fiolia licked her lips in anticipation of a good meal tonight.

Renault nocked the arrow and targeted the bird. *You can do it,* Fiolia thought. Despite their frequent arguments, she and her brother were close.

Renault released the arrow. It struck the ground a few paces from the bird, causing it to flutter away. The Baron chided Renault, whose face was slightly flushed. "Now Fiolia," her father said, "it is up to you to catch our meal for tonight."

They carefully navigated through the forest until they reached a brook. Fiolia could see groups of fish swimming in it. She took aim and drew her bow.

"No," her father said sternly.

"Why father?" she asked, lowering her bow.

"It is too easy, in a real emergency situation you may be leagues from the nearest lake or river. Then what would you do? No. We continue on, for bigger game."

"Not unless we starve to death first," Renault whispered into her ear. Fiolia did her best to squelch a giggle.

After fording the brook they crossed into the woodlands again until they came upon a trench. Fiolia's eyesight was sharp and she swore she saw animal movement, she nocked an arrow and fired into the trench.

"No!" her father said, but it was too late, the arrow struck whatever she had spotted and an explosion tore the trench apart, hurling all three of them backwards. Fiolia cursed her eagerness. *What was that?* Her father brushed himself off and checked on both his children to see if they were alright, while chunks of rock and burnt wood ejected by the blast lay scattered around them.

"You should be more careful, my girl," he said. "Your exuberance nearly cost us our lives." They had suffered some minor bruises and cuts but nothing their Vampire metabolism couldn't handle. Within a few moments their regenerative healing abilities had restored them to full health.

"Father, what was that?" Renault asked.

"Laser mines." The Baron dusted his tunic off and exhaled. "Left over from The last Vaster-Maratak conflict. This forest was once a major battleground between them."

Vampiress remembered her history (for once!) the Vastars had tried to annex this territory from the Maratak Confederacy during the last conflict, while trying to gain control of the Eternal River. Maratak sappers had designed a series of intricate trenches and mined the disputed territory, thus preventing a major Vastar advance. Despite being creatures of light, the Vastars were not as experienced in conventional warfare as the Maratak. The battle had reached an inconclusive stalemate, causing the Vastars to withdraw from the area.

"I guess we can head back to our camp father?" Renault said.

The Baron gave his son a rancorous look but then his face softened. "I am disappointed that you would let one setback come between you and your appetite, but luckily for you two, I brought field rations."

As they made their way back toward the brook, the Baron stopped and listened around him. When

Fiolia saw the look on her father's face she knew something was wrong. "Don't speak Fiolia," he whispered. Up ahead Renault had not noticed that his father had stopped and was surprised when three armored Maratak Patrol Guards suddenly appeared in his path.

"Renault!" the Baron said, not looking the least bit intimidated by the three newcomers, who towered over the surprised Renault.

The three Maratak eyed them suspiciously. "What are you doing here?" the lead one barked. Fiolia figured him for their leader. She placed her hand on the hilt of her dagger but her father grabbed her wrist and shook his head.

"I should ask you the same question."

The Maratak let out a snort, Vampiress could not see its face, protected underneath its battle helm, but its black curved horns featured prominently through the large slits in the sides of its helmet. "This is our territory, Vampire!"

"Since when?" the Baron replied haughtily. "According to our intelligence reports this section is still under arbitration, therefore we claim hunting right privileges as stated in our truce." Fiolia studied the three creatures before her, they looked at one another and spoke in a gruff language before laughing. She hoped her father's arrogant attitude against these three would not get them killed. But Baron Verchase was not a man to be pushed around. That was what worried her.

"That rule is no longer in effect," said the lead Maratak. "So you and your companions will have to come with us, you are all under arrest for espionage!" He nodded to his charges before one of them tried to slap restraining cuffs on Renault. Her brother may not be an expert marksman, but he was lethal with a blade, as soon as the Patrol Guard tried to cuff him he found an opening beneath the Maratak's helm and sliced open its throat. Globs of green blood started rushing from its throat before it dropped the cuffs and cried out.

Fiolia watched as her father ran toward the second Guard. Within the blink of an eye he had grabbed its wrists and hurled it into a tree. But in that time the head Guard had knocked the knife out of Renault's hands and had the boy in a headlock. Fiolia drew her bow and nocked an arrow, the Maratak, having superior eyesight, saw what she was planning and tightened his grip on Renault. "You fire that arrow at me you little cunt and I'll break his neck." Despite possessing Vampire strength, her brother was still no match for a pure-bred Maratak soldier. She found it maddening that again another stalemate had occurred on this accursed land.

"Do it!" Renault said. "Shoot!"

She paused, afraid of hitting her brother.

"Fire the arrow, daughter!" her father urged.

Fiolia froze. It was not like her to have this sort of thing happen to her, she who had been indoctrinated since birth to lead. But now, with her brother's life in her hands, she felt indecisive.

"Remember your training!" her father said. Indeed. She took a deep breath and lined up the Maratak's head inside her bow crosshairs. *I can do this. I can do this.* But before she could release the arrow her father leaped at the Maratak, she released it and it streaked through the air. Her aim would've been true had her father not interfered. He threw himself at the Maratak, who seeing he was caught between the arrow and the Baron, ruthlessly utilized Renault as a live shield. The arrow burst through the boy's throat, tearing it to shreds as bone and gristle flew. The Maratak hurled Renault to the ground right before the enraged Baron grabbed it by the throat and twisted off its head. Fiolia dropped her bow and ran toward her brother's motionless body.

"Renault! Renault!" she cried, tears streaming down her cheeks. She cradled his head as the ground soaked up his blood. Despite his Vampire regenerative abilities the wound he suffered was much too severe, and they were leagues from the closest infirmary. "I'm so sorry!" she said. Renault tried speaking, only gurgled words dripped from his lips, that and thick blood. He tried mouthing something to her as their father looked on, horrified.

She pressed her ear against her dying brother's lips. "It's not your fault," he said, "father….should…not…" A few moments later, he was still. Vampiress returned to the present. She had a mission to complete, and couldn't let her emotions deluge her judgment. Besides, four Sect traitors remained at large in this timeline, on the streets of London, that needed to be eliminated. She cleared her mind, wiped the tears from her cheek and exited the end car.

# Three

*September 8, 1888*

When the second victim surfaced London became gripped by fear.

Robert and Swanson were under fire by Anderson. Unable to pinpoint Nichols' killer they couldn't prevent another woman–Annie Chapman, also a prostitute—from being killed. Her remains had been found by a carman on Hanbury Street. According to the coroner's autopsy she was suffering from syphilis and tuberculosis at the time of her murder.

But this did not ease the situation. Now with London obsessed with the "Leather Apron" killer, Scotland Yard had every Police Constable keeping watchful eyes on any suspicious behavior. The restlessness caused by the two murders resulted in the first arrest of a John Pizer: a Polish Jew who worked in Whitechapel as a bootmaker. An overzealous Police Sergeant named William Thicke was the arresting officer, but Pizer had a strong alibi (he was with relatives at the estimated time of the murder) and was soon released.

Majors had given Robert a new experimental Halogen flashlight, to aid him in his investigation. Robert's only desire was to solve this case.

Unfortunately he would not get his wish.

—⁂—2—⁂—

It was common knowledge Section chief Ambrogio had no love for Vampiress.

One of the main reasons was her father, Baron Verchase who had blocked Ambrogio's promotion to Section Chief twice—due to Ambrogio's lack of aristocratic bloodlines—causing his delay in rising the ranks of The Sect. It was only after he was able to obtain a reprieve by the Viceroy's office that his career was able to resume without hindrance—Ambrogio's second cousin was a close friend of a powerful lord.

So when Vampiress was assigned to his section he felt it appropriate to settle an old wound that ran deep within him. He could not touch the Baron, but with careful planning, his daughter might fall prey to his plan.

But even if she wasn't Verchase's spawn, Ambrogio would find a way to eliminate the woman. She was almost as arrogant as her father, and her insubordination and recklessness had almost jeopardized their mission.

It had all started with the first Whitechapel murder. One of the main reasons for their incursion into this time period of Earth's past.

Ambrogio had ordered her to carry out the executions with particle weapons, but she had (as always) ignored his orders and used her trademark weapons: bow, arrow, and dagger, before finishing off the target in grisly fashion.

Her reason behind this was to avoid detection. But she knew damn well that Humanity possessed no technology capable of detecting an energy signature from an energy weapon. In this reality Earth had only recently entered its industrial age, less than fifty years ago.

What transpired was a pair of grisly killings, drawing the attention of Scotland Yard, and bringing Ambrogio's pristine service record under official inquiry by The Black Arm.

All because of that fucking cunt.

He knew he was in danger of losing his command when ten Hollow Men had been sent to him. Personally he did not care much for these new agents. But The Black Arm was adamant about investigating

Vampiress' activities, so he did not dissent.

"Where is the Vampiress now?" Ambrogio asked one of the newly-arrived Hollow Men. A taciturn fellow (weren't they all?) named Wells, who had neat blonde hair and muscular hands.

Wells stared at Ambrogio and thought for a moment. Ambrogio always found it amusing when their whirlpool eyes began spinning rapidly behind their sunglasses whenever they needed to think or communicate with one another.

"In Knightsbridge district, Chief Ambrogio," Wells replied politely. "Shall I tell her tails apprehend and bring her in for questioning?"

"No, not yet." *Last thing I need is to alert the bitch. If I want to destroy her credentials and send her back in disgrace, I have to plan this right. Her family is too powerful.* "Have them continue to track her movements, but do not move in until I say so." The Hollow Men tracking her were carrying their standard equipment, Black Cubes, capable of transfiguring their appearances into 19th-century London gentlemen. They couldn't go walking around London with those whirlpools now could they?

Vampiress knew she was being followed; the question remaining was who it was. Did Ambrogio have one of his cronies tailing her? Or was it The Black Arm?

She could've easily scanned the area and spotted anyone using a transfiguration device (Black Cubes) but that would've alerted them and then she would be fighting a battle she wasn't ready for. Ambrogio was likely involved, and when she proved it, she would make that worm pay.

Today she had abandoned her cloak and was dressed like a regular Victorian lady. Her wide hat was covered with white and violet plumes, and helped keep the sunlight abated. Not that it would kill her as she was protected by her shield. But she hated wearing the tight undergarments under her day dress; it did not allow for comfortable movement. *How women in this era suffered just to look attractive,* she thought.

Up ahead she saw her quarry. This was one of the main reasons she and her section had been sent to this time period. She had already taken two of them out, now she would track the third before making her move. "You won't escape me," she whispered.

It amazed her how the first two traitors had been easily found and exterminated. Did they think they could escape justice? Vampiress was the top assassin for The Sect, surely they knew of her reputation.

She had never failed in a mission. As a matter of fact she hardly ever missed kills: once she had missed on purpose, that was to frighten off Jackson Mansfield in the alley near Knightsbridge. The other time she had missed it had cost her dearly, her brother Renault.

His death remained an open wound within her. It had also cost her the trust of the academy. It had dropped her after learning of the accident near the Eternal River. Even her father's elevated standing could not get her reinstalled.

But her father would not rest until she was vindicated. Now that Renault was gone it was her responsibility to continue the legacy of their proud family name.

The Baron had enlisted the finest instructors to train her in the arts of physical combat and weaponry. After her daily lessons were over he would continue drilling her until she was exhausted. Not that it bothered her, the extra training helped keep her mind off Renault's tragic death.

With her father's insistence she had been granted probationary standing within the Black Arm. She started as a low-ranking warrant officer. Training fresh recruits from the academy before attracting the attention of the Viceroy's Corps Commander. Once, while observing one of the classes she taught, he had been impressed with her advanced tactical skill. "Where did you learn your skills, Fiolia?" he had asked her.

"From my father, mainly," she had answered.

"I've been told by other high-ranking officials that you shot your brother during a scuffle with Maratak in the forest near The Eternal River."

She knew that he would bring up this topic, her name mired in stigma since the day she had tried to kill the Maratak Patrol Leader. But she knew how to answer her critics. "It was an accident," she said confidently, knowing that would be the only way to win over the Corps Commander. "I have learned from my error, but I will not allow one blemish to prevent me from fulfilling my true purpose of surviving The Sect with distinction."

Indeed, her words had much effect, the next day the Corps Commander awarded her a commission.

From there she began her ascent. Like a Death Angel she terminated every target assigned to her, and won every officer distinction award that existed. The Sect acted as if they had never blacklisted her, instead bestowing upon her the rank of "Field Operations Leader." Now she was their top assassin and finest weapon.

But this was before the Hollow Men had been created by the Black Arm. Despite endowing their new secret police corps with a fierce sense of duty and loyalty, they always sought better ways to accomplish their goals, and the Hollow Men had been their answer.

She turned her attention back toward her target. Amazing how the traitors had blended in with this society. She often wondered why they had chosen this time period. *Perhaps they thought they'd be safe here. But why did they assume identities as female prostitutes?* It had been a long day, and she needed some amusement.

She decided to take a detour and try and lose the two Hollow Men behind her.

That should make Ambrogio angry.

"What a stroke of luck," Jack said. He and McCoy were inside a bookstore when he found a tome about Vlad III, prince of Wallachia, the 15th-century tyrant infamous for impaling his enemies. He purchased the book and went over to McCoy who was trying to locate a book on undead creatures.

"Here we are," said the bookstore clerk, a bushy-haired Irishman with ruddy cheeks and thick grey eyebrows. The title of the book was *Undead Creatures, Volume One*. "Going hunting for goblins again, McCoy?"

Seamus and the clerk were acquaintances; years ago they had both come over from Cork on the same ship. "Same as always."

"Dear God man," the clerk said, "you are a cheeky one, McCoy." Seamus paid the man before he and Jack found a table in the back of the store to inspect the new purchase.

"This book was written by an English professor named Duncan Meadows from King's College. Apparently the book had been published in lieu of Meadows' experience while visiting his father's grave in Sheffield. Apparently he had encountered a ghoul and was successful in killing it. "Meadows claims that the ghoul was living off the land and had attacked sixteen people in Sheffield."

"How did he manage to kill it?" Jack asked. McCoy returned to the tome and after skimming through a few passages. "Just as I thought...silver."

"Will silver help us?"

McCoy closed the book and nodded. "I don't see why not. Ghouls, Zombies, and Vampires are all classified as undead creatures. So, in theory silver should work on all."

"Now all we have to do is find some silver weapons."

McCoy pulled out a revolver and showed it to Jack. "This is an Enfield MK I, it's a .476 caliber gun." McCoy unloaded the bullets from the handgun's cylinder and handed them to Jack.

Jack inspected the bullets. He was expert on ordnance but immediately recognized silver when he saw it. "Where did you have these made?" he handed the silver bullets back to McCoy who reloaded the Enfield and placed it back in his shoulder holster.

"There's a blacksmith up in Manchester who makes all sorts of hard-to-find items." He paused for a moment and lit a cigarette. "When I was on that case up in St. Albans I had it made after I realized I was dealing with Vampires. Now I'll finally get the chance to use it."

Seamus lit a cigarette and the smell of tobacco smoke filled the area around them. Jack checked his pocket watch and realized he needed to get to the hospital; his shift was scheduled to begin within the hour. "I must be leaving you now, Seamus. Duty calls." Seamus stood up and shook Jack's hand. "Stop by the office when you're done with your shift, mate. We can continue our discussion."

Jack smiled. "Not tonight my friend, I have to take my wife to the opera."

That night he took Mercedes to the Royal Opera House in Covent Garden to watch Shakespeare's *Othello*. He was not very fond of these types of productions, and was also tired after his latest shift. But part of marriage was compromise, so he had happily agreed to take her.

They were up in the balcony, overlooking the stage. The play was in the final act and Jack wanted to get a pint at the *Sword & Lion* before heading home. Jack fought hard not to sleep during the performance, but he hadn't slept much in the past few days. Luckily Mercedes was too enthralled with the play to even notice his fatigue. He excused himself and went to stretch his legs, as he stepped off the balcony he saw her.

It was the Vampire woman who had tried to kill him the other day.

She was sitting in one of the boxes watching the play. "Bloody hell," Jack whispered to himself. He didn't know what surprised him more: seeing her here or the fact that Vampires enjoyed opera. He decided he would get a closer look. She wore, a crimson sleeved evening gown with a low-cut bodice. Her dark hair was done up and she would occasionally peek through a pair of binoculars to watch the show.

He found his way to her box and observed her from behind. Around her people were casually viewing the play, unknown that a sinister creature was within their midst. On some foul mission that could spell disaster for England.

He still had the knife she had hurled at him the other day in the alley. He drew it from the inside pocket of his jacket. After twenty minutes she stood up from her seat, lifting her skirts, and came toward him.

This was his chance.

He positioned himself behind one of the curtains, as she exited the box he gripped the knife and rammed his elbow into the base of her skull. The blow knocked her off balance and she stumbled to the ground. At first he felt guilty, having never assaulted a woman before. But this was no ordinary woman. She rubbed the back of her head and quickly collected herself. When she saw him her eyes narrowed into slits and she hissed at him like a serpent. "You again!"

"Here, you forgot this," Jack said, hurling her knife back at her. She moved quickly, It slashed a cut in her sleeve. Despite this she growled at him like a beast and hurled herself at him. He braced himself for impact and felt her body knock him down. Even though he had never wrestled a vampire before he knew her physical strength was superior to that of any ordinary human. They struggled for control until she finally pinned him down.

She barred her fangs at him, and he felt her hot breath. It smelt sweet like cinnamon. "I promise, you will die quickly human," she said, smiling. His wrists were pinned to the red carpet beneath him. She lowered her fangs and he head-butted her. She growled like an injured animal.

"Is there a problem here?" someone said.

Both he and the female Vampire looked up briefly. Two ushers, wearing red uniforms and matching hats had entered the hall, no doubt attracted by the noise Jack and the female vampire had caused during their struggle.

She shot the ushers a smile and straddled Jack. Her skirts were all over his face and when he tried lifting his head up she slammed it down against the floor.

"Get the police!" Jack said.

One of the ushers made a dash for the door. But the Vampire woman was fast, she got to her feet and tackled him. She drew a small knife and slit the usher's throat. Blood spurted everywhere as the young man's fingers tried to stop the torrent of blood draining from his body.

She then hurled the knife at the other usher and it struck the man in the knee.

Jack got up and found the knife she had hurled at him in the alleyway the other day. "You ready for another round, blood-sucker?"

She smiled at him and he braced himself for another assault. But instead of engaging in another round of battle, she lifted up her skirts. "There will be another time," she said. Then she was gone in a blur.

Jack rushed over to the usher whose throat had been cut but the man was still. He felt for a pulse but there was none. He cursed loudly at the senseless death. "This was Nigel's first night on the job," the other usher said sadly. "Poor boy." Jack closed Nigel's eyes and muttered a prayer. Then he pulled out a handkerchief and wrapped the other man's bloody knee tightly.

Robert arrived at the Royal Opera house within twenty minutes. By the time he got there he had four Police Constables alongside him who were still panting from the brisk dash they had endured to keep up with Robert.

Fortunately he had been dining at a fish & chips restaurant in the area so when word reached him of a madwoman who had attacked a man and two ushers in Covent Garden, he dropped his meal and ran as fast as he could. That was when he encountered the four police constables en route.

Inside the main lobby he saw his brother Jack, wearing a tuxedo, treating a man in an usher's uniform. Mercedes was next to him. A crowd of theatre-goers had gathered behind them like a flock of geese. Robert had not expected to see his younger brother, but was glad no harm had come to Jack. "Are you alright?" he asked.

Jack nodded halfheartedly. "Except for my ego."

"She was crazed," the surviving usher said, "and she killed poor Nigel."

Robert turned his attention to a body lying a few feet from where Jack was treating the wounded usher. A white sheet had been placed over Nigel's remains.

Half an hour later a horse-drawn ambulance had arrived to take Nigel's remains away. During that time Jack and the surviving usher, a man named Philip, had given their statements regarding the incident. After Robert had taken down their depositions, Jack asked to speak to him in private, away from the onlookers.

"There is one more thing you need to know about tonight," Jack said.

"You may not believe it, and if you don't, I don't want you to think I'm crazy." Now Robert was insanely curious. "Spit it out, Jack, I'm not in a patient mood."

"The creature that attacked me tonight, and killed that boy, she wasn't human; she was a Vampire."

If they were at a pub or at his home, Robert might've found this amusing. "Quit fucking around, Jack. Dear God man, we've got one dead boy and another man seriously wounded."

"I'm dead serious. This isn't the first time I've seen her. She attacked me in an alleyway outside of Harrods's the other day. Besides, the other night when we were at *The Sword & Lion* weren't you the one who had listened to me when I spoke to you about vampires?"

He did remember. "Why didn't you tell me about this attack before?"

"I went to see a private investigator who deals with these types of cases, besides, you're busy with this 'Leather Apron' killer."

"Is there anything else you're not telling me Jack?" Robert asked, eying his brother suspiciously. He knew when Jack was withholding information.

Jack knew he'd been cornered. "I've been tracking this creature, along with that Irishman, Seamus McCoy. We're both convinced that she's a Vampire, up to no good."

Robert scowled. "You're no detective, Jack; I'm only going to tell you this once, so listen well. Stay the hell out of this case!"

"What you did was quite foolish, Jack; you could've been killed last night."

Jack knew the Irishman was right, but his curiosity had gotten the best of him. "She was right within my grasp, Seamus, what else could I have done?"

"You could've called me; there is a public phone in the opera house you know."

Honestly Jack didn't know of any phones, and he wasn't about to risk losing this Vampire woman while waiting for Seamus to show up. "She's incredibly strong, Seamus, I'm lucky to be alive."

Seamus snorted. "Damn right you are; but now she knows that we're on to her. She may have left town."

"I seriously doubt that. Before she took off she told me 'there will be another time.' No, she's still in London, I suspect we haven't seen the last of her."

"Let's hope you're right, Jack." Seamus handed him today's paper. Jack read the cover story. A local businessman and Baron, Samuel Montague, was offering a reward of £100 for any information leading to the arrest of the Leather Apron killer. "With both this serial killer and our Vampire loose on the streets, it's going to present a challenge to avoid being detected by the police."

# Four

*Blood* rumbled along the track as it left Liverpool Street with its latest cargo.

The new Master Conductor, Lok, had not been happy being assigned this post. Much like his predecessor, he thought it wrong what The Sect was doing to the humans. He felt like a common thief, all this nighttime travel to keep their mission under wraps. No wonder the previous Conductor had rebelled.

His Stoker, Rolfe, was surprisingly quiet about the old Conductor who had mysteriously disappeared. Lok knew that the Black Arm were behind it—they always were: espionage, murders, torture, blackmail. And to make matters worse, more Hollow Men had been posted onboard *Blood*.

He monitored the console and noticed they were approaching the first railroad switch. After that they would accelerate to full speed until they reached the first portal anomaly, which would take them directly to the depot. There, they would unload their impious cargo and start all over again.

When *Blood* had switched tracks, the propulsion computer indicated they needed to accelerate. Lok ordered Rolfe to pick up his pace, slowly *Blood* started accelerating.

Within minutes the red locomotive was moving at flank velocity, the English countryside, bathed in darkness, flew past them as they traveled at speeds not yet possible for human vehicles of this era.

It was now time to activate the portal enhancer, Lok gave the computer a voice command and it responded immediately to his order. Behind the steam dome a small compartment opened and an array rose from inside it. After extending itself, it deployed a powerful yellow beam which streaked ahead like a blazing comet. Within seconds the portal appeared in front of them. It glimmered, matching the color of the beam that had activated it. Via intercom announcement, Lok notified the Hollow Men onboard that they would be passing through the anomaly, back into their own time.

As soon as *Blood* passed through the anomaly the it was enveloped by its energy and transported light years away to a distant planet controlled by The Sect.

Less than a minute later they had arrived. Giant double doors built into a mountain opened beneath a black sky filled with new stars. *Blood* slowed and pulled into the depot. Lok then activated the decontamination filter. After *Blood* cleared security measures, the robotic arms approached the boxcars from both sides and opened their doors.

One by one they removed the canisters, while the Hollow Men supervised the transaction. The canisters glowed through their transparent tops. Most of the colors emanating from them were turquoise, some red, but most were either green or yellow. Lok thought of his own family, and wondered how many human families had been affected by The Sect's quest to regain their homelands. *Do we have the right to destroy another race to regain our old territories?* Lok thought.

After he and Rolfe had disembarked they were approached by two Hollow Men. Lok had no love for these ungodly beings, few did.

"You are almost an hour late," said one of the Hollow Men. He studied Lok, as if trying to get a feel for his response.

"We were delayed," Lok replied. "Vampiress was nearly captured by one of the humans, so we had to wait until we got her approval to depart London."

"Inefficiency will not win the war," the Hollow Man said. Lok felt like ripping off its red sunglasses and ramming it down the creature's throat. He moved his arms behind his back and clenched his fists. "I assure you, my efficiency rating is well within acceptable standards." He wasn't going to have this being tell him he was incompetent, no matter what the situation, he had a reputation to maintain. "If you like I can show you my rating report." Lok pulled out a tiny disc from his overalls' pocket.

The Hollow Man shot the disc a vacuous look. "No. That will not be necessary, carry on, Conductor Lok."

After the Hollow Men had left them Rolfe breathed a sigh of relief. "You really should not test those creatures, or you'll end up like our previous Conductor."

Lok shot Rolfe an agitated look. "Good, then I'll be able to live with myself again."

―2―

The last thing Robert needed was another murder. London was already on edge. He felt the pressure of working alongside Swanson every day and it did not help the situation. Quite the opposite, he found himself trying to prevent additional strain in his working relationship with his superior.

Surprisingly, Swanson had given him a day off to get some rest and relax. After a walk in St. James Park he decided on getting lunch at a local Bavarian restaurant. After traversing Marlborough Road he found himself on St. James Street. The anticipation of a good meal, made him hurry. As Robert approached an old corner warehouse he picked up a smell that reminded him of spoilt food. As he drew closer the smell became worse, and he grew more curious about its origin. The detective inside him decided to investigate. As he approached the structure, he noticed its windows were boarded up. Soon his nose grew accustomed to the smell, but that did not abate his burning desire to learn what was causing it.

A man wearing a strange black suit and tie with a white shirt appeared in a side street adjacent to the warehouse. For some odd reason this person was wearing red- tinted glasses. Robert had never seen anyone dressed in this manner before, except perhaps at a wedding. But even then the red glasses seemed peculiar. "I say ole boy," Robert called out, "do you know what's causing that horrid smell?"

The man ignored Robert and continued on his way. Robert was not anticipating being ignored, nor was he used to it, being a police detective. "Did you hear me?" he yelled. But the man continued his trek and disappeared into the warehouse.

Now Robert was suspicious. He approached the spot where he had last seen the strange man enter the building and found an unlocked iron door.

He opened it slowly and looked inside. The smell was strongest inside, as he had correctly guessed. He drew the experimental halogen flashlight Majors had given him and stepped inside.

Having been a police officer for over a decade, Robert knew when he was in a place of ill-repute. What secrets did this place hold? He thought about calling for backup but it would take time for them to arrive, and he didn't like waiting.

He quietly tip-toed between two rows of stacked crates marked in strange print. For some reason he did not think it was Chinese. His police instincts told him to stop, make notes and leave before…before what? Apart from the strange man the place looked deserted for some time. He ignored the pang of doubt and continued. The smell got stronger, but it no longer reminded him of spoilt food, more like…decomposing bodies.

Not wanting to inhale anymore of this foul air he placed a handkerchief over his mouth and drew his revolver. That was when he spotted the man from outside. He was walking back and forth, carrying what looked like a sack over his shoulder. Robert continued his walk between the rows of crates. As he grew closer he could see that the item the man had slung over his shoulder didn't look like a sack. More like….

"Say!" Robert said. "What in bloody hell is that you're carrying?"

This time the man stopped. He dropped the sack which looked more like a cadaver bag he had once seen in a coroner's office. Robert pointed his weapon at the man. "Alright now, you, hands up! You're going in for questioning."

The taciturn creature did not reply, instead he picked up the cadaver bag and continued with his business. Robert cocked his pistol. "Drop the bag," he ordered.

The man was walking toward what looked like an incinerator. Robert had had enough of being ignored. He fired a warning shot up into the air. The bullet hit the ceiling and ricocheted off the warehouse wall. The man dropped the cadaver bag again and turned to face Robert. "I cannot have you firing your weapon in here," it said calmly. "Now, give me the weapon." It spoke in a condescending tone, like an adult would to a misbehaving child.

"You're not in a position to order me around."

A smirk appeared on the man's chalk face. Robert did not know what the creature found humorous, but he was determined to get answers. The man stretched his arm out. "Give me the weapon," it repeated before closing in on Robert.

"I'm ordering you to stop." Robert pointed the gun at his opponent's knee. He didn't want to kill, only wound. This man obviously was hiding something from him. He fired at the creature's knee. It stopped and pulled the bullet out of its limb before continuing its advance. Robert shook his head.

"Last chance." When the creature took another step, Robert fired point blank. It stopped for a moment pulled the bullet out of its chest and flicked it away as one would flick away a bug.

Robert fired into its head. Three shots. The bullets scored direct hits, and for a moment Robert thought he had halted the creature's advance, but it stopped and pulled the shells out of its face before the wounds on its face sealed themselves. Robert's mouth was agape.

"You cannot harm it, Detective." Robert swiveled around. Standing before him was a dark-haired woman, wearing a violet corset above tight leather breeches and thigh boots. She had a quiver strung over her shoulder and had her bow drawn.

"Who are you people?"

She laughed. "Funny you should ask detective; I had the pleasure of grappling with your brother at the Opera House."

Robert grimaced. *So this is the woman whom Robert had fought.* "If that's the case, then you are under arrest for the murder."

He drew his weapon and she fired the arrow at him. It slammed into his left shoulder and he dropped his weapon, but not before getting a shot off. It missed the woman's head by an inch.

Robert felt his shoulder erupt into a mountain of pain. Blood was everywhere, soon his entire jacket was drenched in blood. He tried reaching for his ankle holster, where he kept his backup gun but the woman stepped on his hand. He grunted. "I'm afraid there is no escape for you, detective. But we will put you to good use before you expire." She spoke to the taciturn being in a strange language Robert had never heard before.

"What is going on here?"

"We're a dying race, detective, and we've learned that humanity has so much more to offer us than blood. Your life force is what brings us here. And I must say that it has proven quite useful."

*What did she mean by life force? Is it our souls they're after?* It was getting harder to concentrate; Robert felt his head grow heavy. The creature picked him up and slung him over its shoulder. The woman followed, the sound of her boot heels echoed throughout the warehouse. "We've been gathering your people and draining them. In turn it has helped resuscitate our people."

His eyelids grew heavier; her voice was slowing, fading into a whisper. "Then there are the needs of our secret police, we call them the Black Arm. They use this life force energy to create the Hollow Men, one of which is carrying you to your final destination."

Robert saw a strange device with flashing lights. People, his people, people from London, were being led to tables that had tubes attached to the strange device. It resembled a sculpture of a bat, wings outstretched, red eyes glowing ominously. The strange creature placed him on a table. The next thing he knew he was being strapped down. Not that he was in any condition to escape. He did not feel the pain from his wound anymore, in fact, he did not feel anything at all. The Hollow Man placed a cone-shaped gadget on his head.

Robert passed out.

⋅⋅−3−⋅⋅

Jack knew something bad had happened to Jack. When Swanson came to visit him at the hospital he worked at he had learned of his brother's disappearance.

Now he had two objectives, stop the Vampire woman, and find his brother. Swanson had told him that Scotland Yard was determined to find Robert and they had dispatched every available Police Constable. He told Jack not to worry.

But how could Jack not worry about his older brother? Robert had been like a father to him after his parents had died. He thanked Swanson, who offered to give him regular updates on the search for his brother.

Mercedes was also devastated by the news as she was quite fond of her husband's charming older brother. Jack did not have much information regarding Robert's disappearance, except that he had had the day off yesterday. He had a feeling that the Vampire was behind it. It was too much of a coincidence to ignore that. Still, he couldn't sit around waiting for his brother to turn up.

He went to see Seamus.

The Irishman was sitting at his desk, reading the daily newspaper when Robert found him. Seamus looked up at smiled. "I was just about to call you Jack, see when we could resume our investigation."

"Robert is missing."

The expression on Seamus' face went from enthusiasm to discontent. "What exactly happened?"

"Do you have any liquor?"

"A bit early for drinking Jack, don't you think?" Seamus poured Jack a glass of Puerto Rican rum. "Now tell me about Robert."

"He's gone missing; when he didn't report to work early this morning his superior became concerned. It's not like Robert to be late to work." Jack took another gulp of rum while Seamus looked deep in thought.

"And you think this Vampire woman has something to do with Robert's sudden disappearance?"

"You read my mind, Seamus."

Seamus did not appear pleased by the compliment. He looked quite concerned about the news Jack had brought to him. "I think we should proceed carefully, it may *seem* like she's involved with Robert's disappearance. Only time will tell. But let's not be rash, we need a plan."

"We must act now; my brother is missing… or worse." Jack did not want to think about the alternatives.

"Unfortunately I'm in no condition to do anything right now." Seamus pulled out a vial filled with milky liquid. "Take this," Seamus said, "may it protect you." He slowly rose from behind his desk and limped toward Jack before handing over the vial.

"What happened?"

Seamus looked at Jack abashedly. "Twisted my ankle, last night, too much alcohol, missed a step, and tumbled down the stairs." He exhaled. "Guess I'm lucky I didn't break my damn neck.

"I guess I am on my own then," Jack said.

"That bottle is filled with garlic powder, if that bitch gets close to you, let her have it. It should cripple her enough for you to take her out." Jack looked at the bottle and reflected on their short-lived partnership. He took out his bill fold and placed some banknotes on the desk. Seamus smiled and handed the money back. "No, Jack this one is on me; now go, find Robert."

Jack shook his friend's hand and left the office. As he left, Seamus muttered a few prayers for the young physician, before sinking back in his chair.

His ankle burned like hell.

# Five

When Jack got home he was surprised to a see a visitor waiting for him in his living room, sitting across from Mercedes drinking coffee. When he stood up to greet Jack he looked like a giant. His guest spoke with a thick Welsh accent.

"My name is Rowan Majors," he said. "Your wife was kind enough to host me until you arrived. I work with your brother Robert. Did he ever mention me?"

*Knew? Why does he assume Robert is already dead?* "Robert seldom spoke about his co-workers when he was off duty. What brings you here Mister Majors?"

Mercedes saw this as her cue and excused herself.

"I wanted to check and see how things were here," Majors said, "and I wanted to see if there was anything I could do to help."

Jack was touched that this bear of a Welshman was volunteering his services. "I don't see how you *can* help, Mr. Majors."

Majors smiled, and when he did his square jaw revealed a set of straight, ivory teeth. "Jack, I work in the experimental division of Scotland Yard. I design experimental weapons and advanced countermeasures to help safeguard the well-being of our police force.

"Listen, I know Swanson visited you earlier, I know the man, while he is a competent police detective he is also a slave to the bureaucratic ways of the justice system." Majors paused a moment to clear his throat.

"So what are you trying to tell me?" Jack said.

"As much as Swanson wants to find Robert, alive, he is also under pressure to solve the case. This 'Leather Apron' killer case has taken its toll on Scotland Yard. And now Robert's disappearance has added to that. What I'm trying to say is that Swanson's first priority is to find the killer; everything else, is secondary."

Jack wasn't surprised. If he was in Swanson's position he would probably focus all his resources into solving the case. "Swanson told me he has assigned a unit to find Robert."

Majors sighed. "Well, I'm sure he's got someone scouring the city looking for your brother, but it's probably not a 'unit.' Swanson knows his priorities and had to make a token appearance out of respect to

Robert. He didn't want to give you any further cause to worry."

Jack nodded. "So you said you wanted to help me?"

"Yes. I can design a weapon for you. You wife told me that you hired a private investigator to help you track down the individual you think is a *vampire*."

Jack didn't know why Mercedes spilled the news, especially to a man working for Scotland Yard. Majors must've convinced her somehow. Still, Majors did not strike Jack as the type to come here and offer to help if he was going to report Jack to Swanson. "My wife has an active imagination."

Majors leaned in closer toward Jack, and he saw the serious look in the Welshman's eyes. Jack decided he would trust this man. "Perhaps she does, but I wouldn't be surprised if your quarry was whom your wife claims her to be."

"There is, perhaps something you *can* do for me, Mr. Majors.

Majors pulled out a small pad and pencil from the inside pocket of his jacket and Jack told him exactly what he needed.

They went upstairs. Jack took Majors into the attic before opening up an old trunk that held items from his service in the Boer war of 1880. His old military uniform was still neatly folded inside. Atop it sat his old sun helmet which he had worn when he served in the 4th Battalion, which was the King's own Royal Lancaster Regiment. He pulled out his sabers and drew one from its scabbard. "Can you coat these blades with silver?"

Majors took the sabers and inspected them. "I don't see why not. Is there anything else Jack?"

He handed Majors the snuff bottle. "This was given to me by a friend. It's garlic essence. Is there any way you can turn this into a weapon for me?"

"I don't see why not. Maybe I can create a sort of mechanism where the contents can be delivered into the air, like a spray."

"How soon can I have these?"

Majors thought it over for a few moments. "Within forty-eight hours, I would say."

Jack thought that was reasonable enough time to get prepared for his ordeal. "Very well then, I'll see you soon." After Majors had left Mercedes came up into the attic where Jack was looking through his other trunks to see if he could find anything useful to use against his vampire enemy.

"Jack? What's going on?" she asked, looking frightened.

He paused with his task. "Just work love."

"I'm worried Jack, what are you planning to do?"

"I'm going after Robert; I have to find him."

Mercedes took his hand and he saw the tears welling up in her brown eyes. "Jack, this is a police matter, maybe you shouldn't get involved."

"Nonsense." He resumed his work.

"Jack, I don't want you to do this; you could get killed."

She was right. But what other options did he have? He couldn't stand by idly while his brother was still missing. "He's my family, Mercedes."

"So am I," she pleaded. "And there is one more thing you need to know. I'm pregnant with our first child."

He looked up at her and they embraced. "A baby?" He had no idea she was carrying his child. It was a bittersweet feeling, knowing that he would become a father. And as much as he wanted to live to see the birth of his son or daughter he would never be able to rest until he knew what had happened to Robert. "I don't know what to say, Mercedes. Of course I am overjoyed, but I cannot sit around and wait for Robert to turn up."

She lowered her head. As if she understood that he would not change his mind. "I just don't want my baby to grow up without a father." He kissed her on both cheeks, then embraced her again, hoping he would live to witness the child's birth.

*-2-*

Almost two weeks passed since Jack had learned he was to become a father. Despite his efforts he had made little headway in finding the vampire woman or Robert. As much as he hated to admit it, the possibility of finding Robert alive was becoming slim. Majors had kept his promise, and had delivered his sabers with new silver blades in addition to the garlic spray. Jack was itching for the opportunity to use both these weapons against the Vampire. He had also started a vigorous exercise regiment to get in shape and had asked for a leave of absence from his medical residency. It was reluctantly granted.

London was soon faced with another dilemma. In addition to the two Whitechapel murders, an alarming number of London citizens had also disappeared. Men, women and children from all walks of life simply vanished. The reports were alarming, and now Scotland Yard was faced with yet another crisis.

Every night he was on the streets of London. Armed with sabers and garlic spray. Seamus had also loaned him his revolver with the silver bullets. During his nightly sojourns, he wore a top hat and covered his mouth with a thick scarf to conceal his identity. It made him look suspicious but he did not see any other way around it. If he wanted to continue his clandestine operations, this was the way to do it.

His activity was also taking a toll on Mercedes. She had grown distant, and Jack could not blame her. He knew she felt as if he had chosen Robert over her and the baby. He found himself thinking more about the child with each passing day.

When September 27th arrived London's Central News Agency received a letter titled "Dear Boss" signed by someone called "Jack the Ripper."

Jack felt as if a boulder had fallen on him. The killer was now calling himself Jack. He didn't know if it was pure coincidence, or if someone was trying to frame him. He guessed the later, he must be getting closer to finding his vampire nemesis. Was this her way of fighting back?

Then, on September 29th he was scouring the streets at night near the area where the first two murders had transpired. His suspicious dress attracted the attention of a Police Constable. Jack was lucky to have outrun him, otherwise it would've been difficult explaining himself, armed and dressed as he was. September 30th arrived. That night two more women were murdered. Both within an hour of one another. The first, Elizabeth Stride, another prostitute, was found by a jewelry dealer named Louis Diemschutz in Dutfield's yard. The second woman, Catherine Eddowes, was found by Police Constable Edward Watkins in Mitre Square.

Now Jack found himself in an even more precarious position. Would he continue his nocturnal forays, and risk detection again? Or possibly capture? With the killer identified as 'Jack' he would no doubt be a prime suspect in the murder investigation. He cursed his luck.

Mercedes had already left London and returned to her family in Spain. How could he blame her? He hadn't been a good husband to her since he had started his missions, leaving her alone, now he suffered what she must have while he was out searching for Robert and the mysterious Vampire woman who had twice tried to kill him.

There was a knock at the door. Jack wasn't expecting anyone; he got up to see who is was.

When he opened the door Swanson was standing in his doorway. Behind him were two Police Constables.

※-3-※

"Good morning Dr. Mansfield," Donald Swanson said.

Jack felt a mite of apprehension but did not let it show. "Detective Swanson, what brings you here?"

"Just to ask a few questions, may I come in?"

The last thing Jack wanted was to have these three men inside his home. He hadn't even had time to tuck away his sabers and clandestine attire which he wore during his twilight treks. Swanson noticed his hesitation. "Please, Doctor, it will only take a few minutes."

To spurn Swanson would only elicit further suspicion, and there was nothing preventing them to return later with more men. He opened the door wider to admit the trio of men. "Of course, please come in."

He offered them tea and they politely declined. With the token pleasantries out of the way Jack prepared himself for Swanson's interrogation.

"Doctor I would like to talk to you about something."

"Have you found Robert?" Jack asked, knowing quite well they hadn't.

"Unfortunately not, but that is not why I'm here." The two constables broke away from Swanson. Jack eyed them suspiciously as they looked around his living room, meticulously inspecting the cocktail and end tables like they were suspects. "I wanted to talk to you about your nightly activities."

*So. He did know about it. Swanson was definitely a shrewd detective.* But how did he find out? He decided to play the honesty game for as long as he could.

"Why yes, I do go out from time to time for my brisk walks. Does my nightly exercise present some sort of problem?"

Swanson's grey eyes studied him for a moment. "Not if they don't interfere with police business, Doctor."

"I don't understand, Detective Swanson."

Swanson nodded to his two officers who disappeared from the living room. One went into the kitchen, the other headed upstairs. "What is the meaning of this? Am I to assume you have a proper search warrant for scouring my home?"

"If a search warrant will put you at ease, doctor, I'm sure I can obtain one."

Jack knew Swanson was aware his search of the premises was illegal. But how could he prove it? Besides, Swanson was right. He could always return with an official search warrant, but then Jack would become a prime murder suspect; he might even be arrested.

Swanson took out a small note pad and looked it over. "You were spotted leaving your house the night of September 30th. What were you doing outside your home, doctor?"

"As I stated earlier, simply taking my walk, Detective Swanson."

The constable that had gone upstairs returned. He was carrying Jack's two sabers. "Found these upstairs in his bedroom, boss."

Swanson's brows tightened when he saw the two weapons. "Do these belong to you, Doctor?"

"Yes."

"Might I ask what you are doing in possession of such weapons?"

"I served in the Boer war in 1880."

Swanson meticulously scribbled notes down on his pad. Jack did not like where this investigation was going. Regardless, he kept calm. The other police constable emerged from the kitchen a few moments later. He padded up to Swanson's side like a guard dog. "Nothing in the kitchen, sir." "That's fine, I have enough for now." Swanson turned back towards Jack. "Doctor, are you aware that it looks a bit odd to be taking walks late at night carrying weapons of this sort? Especially in unsafe areas where murders have been committed?"

Was Swanson trying to entrap him with that accusation? He and the two PCs eyed him like hungry tigers, ready to pounce. Perhaps Swanson did have some sort of surveillance in place, and Jack had been unlucky (or careless) enough to fall prey to it. He decided to play it safe. "You're quite correct, Detective. I have been in possession of my two sabers when I have ventured out at night."

"May I ask why?"

Jack leaned back and stretched his legs out. "Why it's like you said, Detective, those areas I've been spotted in are quite unsafe, and as I value my life I felt I would be best served carrying proper protection in the event someone was to threaten me."

For a moment Swanson was silent. Jack did his best to conceal his mirth, he had beaten Swanson at his own game of questioning, using facts provided by Swanson himself to corroborate his actions. Swanson stood up and the two police constables fell in behind him. "Dr. Mansfield, I bid you good day. But this will be your only warning: stay out of this case, failure to do so will result in your arrest."

After Swanson and his men had left Jack started making plans for his next foray, but first, he needed to visit Seamus.

―4―

Ambrogio had had enough of Vampiress. He decided today would be the day he made his move. Then Baron Verchase would be short a daughter, and he would be rid of one major problem. The incident at the warehouse had been the last straw. She had allowed an English detective to discover their production facility and uncover their operations. What would've happened if he has gotten away and alerted Scotland Yard? Then their incursion into this time period would've been jeopardized. But Ambrogio's patience had paid off; he had built a solid case against Vampiress. Now was the time to act.

He summoned four Hollow Men into his office. "The time has come to apprehend Vampiress. You all have your instructions." The lead Hollow Man named Krill nodded. "What if she resists?"

Ambrogio repressed a smile. "Then leave nothing to chance; kill her. And make sure you set fire to the warehouse; make it look like an accident. It's already attracted attention once. We'll just have to set up in another location. This will cost us time and resources, but, we'll be rid of its incriminating evidence *and*

Vampiress' incompetence. Contact me when you've completed your mission."

Krill nodded and gathered three more Hollow Men before leaving Ambrogio's office. After they left Ambrogio took out his tablet and began composing a report to Sect Command.

※5※

When Robert awoke from his coma, he wished he hadn't.

Around him were other prisoners. Like him they were strapped in harnesses suspended by thick cords. Transparent tubes, attached to their limbs, fed into a strange device that resembled an immense water tank. He tried moving but found himself tightly snared, like a fly caught in a spider's web.

How long had he been out? Hours? Days? Weeks? His last memory was confronting the man carrying the cadaver bag and the strange woman that Jack had mentioned. He wondered if his colleagues had dispatched search parties to try and locate him. Even if they eventually found him, it might be too late.

He tried moving his head around but his neck was sore. He did manage to get a closer look at his limbs. The skin on his arms and legs had patches of violet bruises that hadn't been there before his capture. He did not know what was worse, being strung up helplessly, like a slab of meat, or knowing he had failed in his duty.

Beneath him the strange creatures in black suits loitered around. Some stood guard near doorways, others were hunched over consoles with flashing lights. He thought he heard someone call them 'computers,' whatever those were. Despite being indisposed, he still could think. He had to use his experience so he could help the people around him. Robert felt a weight in his trouser pocket, it was his knife. They had stripped him of his jacket, socks, shoes and shirt, but hadn't bothered checking his trousers. If he could just reach it he might be able to sever the tubes plugged into his arms and legs. The more he looked at them, the more restless he grew. It felt as if they were sucking the life out of him. And maybe they were. He heard the swish of an opening door and saw the strange woman with dark hair below him enter the chamber. She walked with a type of superiority that bordered on haughtiness. Robert thought he read an expression of contempt on her face when she interacted with the strange creatures in dark suits and red shirts.

His stomach felt queasy, and he felt he would vomit, yet he didn't. *How can I when I haven't eaten?* But he couldn't stay here and wait for death. He had to try escape, even if it cost him his life. If he stayed here, he'd die anyway. He breathed deeply and summoned his remaining stamina.

He tried grasping one of the cords that restrained him. The harness strapped to his chest tightened. No. He had to try another approach. This time he thought through the situation from a different angle. The strange creatures beneath him paid no attention to him or the others. *They don't see us as a threat,* he thought. *And why should they? We're their prey.* Perhaps he could use their overconfidence against them.

He twisted his head around to get a look around and spotted a landing coiled around the side of the warehouse. If he could swing himself over to the railing he might be able to shake himself free, and with the knife cut through his tube bonds.

Again he channeled his remaining strength into escape. He started jerking around like a lobster caught in a fisherman's net until he began swinging. Not enough to reach the landing, but enough to get some momentum going. He took a quick look below, those strange blokes in the suits and red glasses were still not paying heed to him or the others.

He tried swinging again. This time he bumped into a woman with yellow saggy skin. Her body gave off an odor that reminded him of rubbing alcohol. This would be his fate if he didn't escape his predicament. He made another attempt at reaching the railing and managed to get one foot around a pylon. It felt cold against his foot, and he was in danger of sliding free before he twisted his ankle around and hooked it. *I've got to make this work.* The tubes attached to his legs made traction difficult. But with one strong jerk he managed to free his foot from the tube. A current of static electricity shot through his leg before some yellow-pus fluid leaked from the tube.

For a few moments his leg felt numb. He struggled to hold on to the railing with his other leg while he yanked his arms free of the other tubing. More liquid ejected from them, and this time it smelled like wet paint. Robert looked at his arms. They were discolored, a mixture of yellow and violet bruises and welts where the tubes had been attached. He spent a minute recuperating from his ordeal. His limbs were weak, but he was able to walk, perhaps, in time he would regain full strength. For now, his only thought was to find a way out of this warehouse and get help.

He watched for any sign of activity before tiptoeing across the landing, his bare feet upon the cold floor.

# Six

Krill did not understand the concept of emotion; being a Hollow Man he had none.

The Section Chief, Ambrogio, was a different matter. Krill could tell Chief Ambrogio had no love for the Vampire woman named Vampiress. He made it clear by his manner. To Krill ambition was an alien concept; emotion a weakness. To allow one's senses to be manipulated could prove costly, especially in his line of work. He had more important things to do.

He turned his thoughts to his current task, the elimination of Vampiress. He had studied her file, she had an impressive kill ratio. According to The Sect database she had never failed a mission. Ambrogio was putting himself in an arduous position by opposing her. But Krill figured the Section Chief knew what he was doing. Either way he had a mission to complete.

Under a shroud of protection, he and his associates traveled undisturbed. Their holographic physical images altered to make them appear as late-19th-century London gentlemen. This way they could travel without revealing their true appearance.

The streets were packed with four-legged beasts hauling carts and carriages. A few crude-looking vehicles propelled by internal combustion plodded alongside them. Krill figured these vehicles had only been invented recently, they certainly struggled to accelerate toward higher speeds.

When they reached the warehouse, they triggered the defense perimeter and within moments they were confronted by one Hollow Man watcher. Unlike Krill and his companions, this Hollow Man was not dressed in the trademark black suit and red shirt worn by elite Hollow Men. Instead it wore a simple white shirt under its black suit and tie, which designated its Watcher status.

"State your purpose here," said the Watcher, who was also concealed under a holographic image. But Krill's eyes could see the watcher's true form. No Hollow Man was obfuscated to another.

"Arrest and detention," Krill responded.

"There must be a mistake," the watcher replied. "Or else I would've been alerted."

If Krill had an ego he might've found this comment offensive, instead he drew his black cube. It projected his written orders in holographic format to the watcher who read it and nodded.

"Follow me." The watcher led Krill and his four charges through the security checkpoint. Through his red sunglasses his whirlpool eyes scanned the area. Dozens of Hollow Men were congregated near the checkpoint. They were all heavily armed: electric flails, disintegrators, hand scythes, rippers. All impressive weapons, but none carried Black Cubes, the most dangerous weapon bestowed upon Hollow Men.

He had no desire to go to war with his brethren, but if they opposed him and his charges, what else could he do? Negotiation was never part of this mission, nor was it programmed into his psyche.

After passing through the checkpoint Krill scanned the area, trying to locate Vampiress. His men would also be at work conducting the same search.

"Unauthorized scanning is prohibited in this area," the Watcher said. "And I must also ask that you relinquish your Black Cubes, before proceeding inside the facility."

Krill did not have to explain himself to this automaton, whose programming was limited in scope. Having succeeded in gaining access to the warehouse, he was ready to proceed with his mission.

He nodded at his four charges; they drew their Black Cubes and fired into the remaining Watchers, vaporizing them before they could draw their weapons.

Krill grabbed the lead Watcher by the throat and with one quick jerk tore off its head. The Watcher's eye glasses dropped to the ground; its whirlpool eyes stared surprisingly at Krill before fading.

With their opposition neutralized, they proceeded.

Inside her office, Vampiress was looking over some reports pertaining the energy transfusions when she realized something had gone wrong. The checkpoint security monitors were offline. When she attempted communications with the security personnel there was no response. *What is going on there?*

What made the situation even more strange was that it was unlike the Hollow Men to ignore her. While they didn't fawn over her every request, they were efficient and that was why she had requested them for this assignment. Not one to take chances she donned her armor and grabbed her weapons.

She had a feeling she would need them.

Krill was expecting more resistance from his opposition. With the exception of two defense drones he and his forces had met no resistance. It was unfortunate that theHollow Men at the checkpoint had to be destroyed but that was the nature of this mission. It was not like The Sect to leave a vital transfusion depot without adequate defenses, even if it was stationed in a technologically inferior era.

Krill and his team passed through a corridor before encountering the last checkpoint leading to the transfusion chambers. Only one Watcher stood guard.

"State your purpose," the lone Watcher said. It was dressed similarly to the previous watcher, a white shirt under its black suit. Krill removed his Black Cube and fired into the watcher's chest, it disintegrated, but not before sounding the alarm. Klaxons tore through the building, alerting its occupants that it had been compromised.

Krill had his work cut out for him.

After the klaxon sounded Vampiress located another monitor and was greeted by the five intruders advancing through the depot. They were definitely not her men, they were Elites, Ambrogio must have sent them. So, Ambrogio had played his hand. Now it was her turn to return the favor.

On the security monitor, two of her Watchers were attempting to keep the redshirts at bay near the entrance of the transfusion chamber. They fought valiantly, but up against five Elite Hollow Men armed with Black Cubes, even the fiercest Watcher could not match that firepower. They succumbed to the intruders.

She punched in her security code and waited for the retina scan to admit her into the south entrance of the transfusion chamber.

Her remaining white-shirt Hollow Men were rushing toward the scene of the main battle. She hoped they could slow the obtruding force that threatened to destroy all she had worked for.

She heard the destructive sounds of Black Cubes, vaporizing any opposition in their way. Vampiress did not fear these weapons; she had faced long odds before.

She still could not see the red shirts. There were far too many obstructions before her: terminal bulkheads, canisters, and transfusion tanks. She nocked one of her arrows and located a vantage point where she would have the high ground.

This battle was only just starting.

When Robert heard the alarm go off his eardrums pounded against the side of his temples. Had he been discovered? If that was the case then how come he still had not been apprehended?

His strength was slowly returning, no doubt the separation from the tubes plugged into his limbs had aided his recovery.

From where he was standing he could see the five newcomers spreading destruction wherever they went. They resembled the chalk-faced creatures stationed here, but wore red shirts instead of white. In a strange way Robert found that interesting.

The intruders were too busy fighting off their opposition to notice him. Being on an elevated landing, he had the advantage of witnessing the events below him. But he had to find a way to escape so he could come back and help free the people trapped here.

One of the newcomers fired at the creatures beneath him, vaporizing it. Despite having superior numbers, the creatures guarding the facility were being overwhelmed by the five red-shirted newcomers.

Discarded weapons littered the floor beneath him. Robert knew he had to get his hands on one if he was to escape, but how? To step onto the battlefield beneath him would be suicide.

He found a stairwell that led downstairs and slid down the banister. When he reached the ground floor he took cover behind a pylon and scoured the area fora weapon. A few steps from him were the disintegrated remains of one of the creatures; near it a weapon resembling a guisarme. On its blade were strange inscriptions. He bolted toward it and picked it up. Upon grasping its shaft the blade lit up and without warning it fired an electrical projectile that took out an entire panel across from where he stood. Robert did not know how he had activated it but after eying its shaft he noticed row of small buttons, each a different cover. He must've accidentally pressed one. Now his chances of escape had improved.

He saw two dangling bodies come undone from the rafters and fall onto the row of canisters below. The glowing lights emanating from the canisters ceased and Robert wished he could fish out the bodies. But crossfire from two sets of opposing combatants made that a mission too hazardous to undertake.

He heard the swish of elevators door open and saw the Vampire woman. She was armed with a bow and a quiver of arrows slung over her back. He took up a defensive position and pressed another button on the shaft of his guisarme. A wide burst of projectiles exploded from the blade and plowed into the panel above the elevator door where she had stood, showering her with white sparks that bounced off her armor.

Not knowing where her attacker was, she hit the floor before unleashing an arrow that found its mark into the chest of one of the red-shirted creatures.

She fired a volley in Robert's direction. The arrows found their mark in the warehouse's wall and exploded. A loud explosion rocked the impact area before Robert felt the weight of the wall come crashing down on him.

Vampiress did not know who had fired the guisarme at her, but she didn't think it could've come from one of her Watchers. First, they rarely turned against their superiors, second, the aim was off, not intrinsic behavior for Watchers, creatures known for their expert marksmanship.

Much to their credit her defenders were fighting dauntlessly, despite being out-matched by superior firepower. Around her dusty remains of disintegrated Watchers littered the floor. Wounded Watchers not destroyed by Black Cubes lay still, their faces solemn; eye-sockets once active with whirlpool vision now resembled dark cave openings. Ambrogio would pay for this outrage.

"Vampiress!" said a voice. It was so powerful its broadcast could be heard over the sounds of battle. The voice's owner shouted her name three more times before she ordered her surviving Watchers to cease fire.

A few seconds later a tall, broad-shouldered Hollow Man appeared. "I call for temporary cease-fire," it said. Despite the destruction and carnage around it, its suit looked freshly-pressed, as if it had just been cleaned.

"I agree to terms," she replied. Not really wanting to treat with this Hollow Man, but perhaps she could buy time for herself.

The Hollow Man raised his hands to indicate he was unarmed. That did not mean much to Vampiress, who had fought against foes who were adept at deception, this opponent was no different.

She rose to meet him, in the center of what was once a prime depot. Now a section of it lay in ruin.

Vampiress had never fought against Hollow Men before, especially the new elite forces which were used exclusively by the Viceroy himself. But for what it was worth, her Watchers had acquitted themselves admirably in battle.

"I am Field Operator Krill; Chief Ambrogio sent me to arrest you."

*I was right. It was Ambrogio.* "On what charge?" she asked calmly.

"Reckless endangerment of the mission; according to Chief Ambrogio your actions warrant termination of your field command, effective immediately. Afterwards you will be transported to the Archipelago system where you will be arraigned at Sect Command."

She knew Ambrogio better than he knew her. He would never allow her to be transported back alive to headquarters. Didn't he know how powerful her family was? *Of course he did.* "And if I refuse?"

Krill did not appear daunted by her alacrity. "Then you shall be executed immediately." He reached into his jacket pocket to draw something when Vampiress made her move.

⋆2⋆

She pulled the detonator from inside her corset and armed it. Her father had given it to her years ago, in the event that she faced a situation as dire as this, and she was grateful he had.

She had only a few moments before it would detonate, leaving half of the structure in ruin, but it was the only way to ensure total destruction of the Elite Hollow Men. Her own men would be destroyed as well, but she was willing to pay that price in order to escape to.

As she had anticipated, Krill had drawn his Black Cube. In a way she admired the ruthless streak of these new Hollow Men. Behind her she heard the sounds of the cubes death rays. To their credit, her charges had resumed firing on Krill and his associates, they would buy time for her escape.

She hit the ground and rolled. Activating her transport device, she reappeared at a safe distance outside the warehouse.

It was time to pay Ambrogio a visit.

Robert's forehead was bleeding, but, he was grateful to still be alive. He slowly removed himself from the rubble. His arms and legs were lacerated with cuts and bruises, and he felt pain throbbing through his ribcage, but otherwise he was able to resume his escape.

He saw the Vampire woman confronting one of the strange red-shirted creatures and had kept his cover behind an overturned support beam. He saw her conversing with one of them, a tall broad-shouldered fellow with glossy brown hair that was slicked back over its skull. The creature had drawn something from his jacket pocket, and that was when the Vampire woman had countered by hurling a small metallic device to the ground before disappearing. *Where did she go?*

Robert had no idea what the item was. From where he was situated it resembled a small pyramid-shaped device with flashing lights. The lead creature that had confronted the vampire woman was shouting orders to his troops, causing the redshirts to retreat from the vicinity of the flashing object. Robert limped as fast as he could through the torn warehouse wall, till wondering where the vampire woman had disappeared to. Moments later, behind him, there was more shouting, then a loud explosion. The ground beneath him shuddered and he was hurled into the air like an acrobat. His body felt like a falling meteor before he somersaulted and crashed one block from where he had stood a moment ago. For the second time in one day bits of rubble and refuse rained down on him like hail. Against the odds, he had survived another violent explosion.

After peeling himself off the pavement, Robert spat out the metallic taste of his blood. Touching his cheek he felt the gash that had sliced it open when he had landed on the sidewalk. He eyed the smoldering ruins of the warehouse.

Half of it was gone.


When Vampiress appeared inside her room, back at Section headquarters, she wasted little time. The building's sensors would soon detect her appearance and alert Ambrogio, so she had to work fast if she was to take him by surprise.

She pulled out a thin case from under her bed. Inside was her prized weapon, a bow her father had given her after she had been reinstated by the academy. She armed herself with disintegrator arrows (the only weapon that stood chance of proving effective against Hollow Men) and left her room.

Krill had yet to check in when Ambrogio realized something had gone wrong.

Elite Hollow Men were supposed to be indefatigably efficient, but he had lived long enough to know that no one was perfect.

He drew his sword and exited the office. That was when the proximity alarm went off. He tried his communicator. The frequency used by the Watchers was eerily quiet. He checked the bandwidth to see if it was operational, it was, there just wasn't anyone sending or receiving messages.

Of the three watchers that guarded the corridor where his office was located, only one remained. A fellow named Drek whose eyes swirled relentlessly behind his sunglasses.

"Report!"

"An unauthorized teleport was detected; Mur and Foy went to investigate." Drek grasped his pole-axe and its energy blade fed off of his anxiety, emitting an erratic pulse. Ambrogio knew the Hollow Men's weapons responded to their state-of-mind. But he had never seen one like this. They were supposed to be devoid of emotion, yet Drek looked uneasy, if that was possible for a Hollow Man.

"Which direction did they go?"

Drek swallowed hard. "Level 5." That was where Vampiress' quarters were located. Shit. *The bitch must've survived.*

"Summon the rest of the men," Ambrogio said. "Anyone you can spare."

"As you wish Chief, but that will take time; most of the watchers are locked out of the building."

*Another setback.* "When were you going to tell me this?" Ambrogio said.

Drek bypassed the question. "After the intruder teleported into the building, a message was sent to secure the outside of the building. Your emergency code was used."

"I issued no such order."

Drek nodded. "Yes, we figured this out, only that was after the majority of our forces had been lured into the stratagem."

*Cunning little bitch. But she won't get better of me.* "Follow me." Ambrogio had one more move to make, and he wasn't about to let Vampiress succeed.

Not on his watch.

The first action Vampiress took after she had armed herself was sending a false alert of an external threat.

She wanted to throw the Watchers off track after the internal sensors had detected her presence. Using her vast knowledge of command codes, she had tricked the computer into thinking Ambrogio had sent it.

That had bought her precious time, but she still met resistance in the hallway. Two watchers had ordered her to drop her weapon and stand down, her response had been to drop them instead—two disintegrators arrows right in their chests.

She found the arsenal and armed herself with an energy shield that could absorb a multitude of weapon fire from opposing forces. There were no Black Cubes, of course they were the deadliest weapon available and were under heavy guard in a clandestine chamber only Ambrogio had access to.

She heard a noise outside. It was the pulsing sound of an energy field being activated. She looked and saw that two fields had been activated, boxing her in the corridor. She fired an arrow at one of the shields, destabilizing it for a few moments before she was able to pass through.

She checked one of the terminal panels and saw that the trapped Hollow Men were still outside. But they were ingenious creatures, and would soon find away to override the lock-out.

The hallway lights began flickering like fireflies, no doubt the building's main power was being rerouted. They finally went out before the emergency lights kicked in, shrouding Vampiress in a hazy amaranth hue.

The Elevator doors at the end of the hall opened and two technicians greeted her with fearful glances. She ordered them to stay where they were and they acquiesced. It was risky keeping them alive, the possibility remained they could betray her location, but she had a bigger problem to consider. The main being Ambrogio. She located a teleportation closet and found that there was enough power for one transport. She programmed her destination and stepped into the teleportation tube.

Ambrogio and Drek headed to the Black Room. The infamous facility which only Section Chiefs had access to.

After the retina scan, Ambrogio was granted access. He allowed Drek to follow him inside the room. Ambrogio then located the armory where the Black Cubes were located. He handed one to Drek, who tossed aside his pole-axe.

"It appears your brethren have managed to reroute power and use it to overload the master computer." Ambrogio pointed to the readout on one of the monitors, Drek nodded, the whirlpools in his eye-sockets grew active, resembling cyclones.

"Order them to the Black Room," Ambrogio said. Drek's whirlpools ceased for a moment while he relayed their location to the other Hollow Men.

"I'm afraid you're too late."

*That voice. But how?* Before Ambrogio could draw his Black Cube he felt a sharp object pierce his wrist. His hand dropped to the floor as blood spurted from his wrist. He gritted his teeth when Vampiress emerged behind a computer terminal. He cursed and waved his bloody stump angrily at her. "You!" he said, turning to Drek. "Kill that bitch!"

But Drek stood in his spot, motionless.

Ambrogio did not know why his charge was not responding to his orders.

"Didn't you hear me?" he hissed. "I said kill that fucking bitch!"

"It's no use, Ambrogio," Vampiress said. "I was able to deactivate their command functions. It was quite simple, once I gained access to this room of course."

Ambrogio cursed his luck. She must've used some sort of program loophole to get through the Black Room's security net when main power went out. Not an easy task, but he had underestimated her technical skill with computers. Still, he had one last play to make. "Computer," he said. "Commence self-destruct sequence. Command code: Ambrogio."

The computer's voice came alive and asked for the remaining pass codes. Ambrogio spat out a sequence of codes before countdown commenced. "Now the game is over, Vampiress." Ambrogio smiled. "Your arrogance has doomed you again. First, your brother, now you! Your father will have no heir to carry his line."

Vampiress returned his smile. "I doubt that." She turned toward Drek. "As you already know, Ambrogio, in the event of the Section Chief being rendered implacable, Hollow Men have been programmed with the necessary subroutines to take command. And since you haven't changed *their* pass code, I was able to. Drek," she said in an authoritative voice, "deactivate the self-destruct sequence. Command code: Vampiress Override One."

Drek's eyes became active again and seconds later the countdown ceased. "Now Drek," Vampiress said as Ambrogio looked on dejectedly, "eliminate Chief Ambrogio. Command code: Vampiress Override two."

Drek drew his Black Cube and aimed it at Ambrogio, who muttered a series of expletive at Vampiress before he was blasted into oblivion.

When the remaining Watchers arrived at the scene, they were confronted by their new Section leader. Vampiress ordered them to clean up Ambrogio's remains and dump it in the back alley. No one dissented.

※ 3 ※

When Lok learned of the coup d'état at section headquarters he did not question it. He would be fooling himself if he thought it was not inevitable. Everyone assigned to this mission knew of the strained relationship between Ambrogio and Vampiress. From a neutral standpoint it was only a matter of time before the struggle played itself out.

He would do his best to please his new leader. He knew what Vampiress was capable of, to oppose her would condemn him to an early grave; he had a family to think about.

He was a moderate, with no love for extremist politics. Having been forced into his position he would be glad when this assignment was over. Not all Vampires from the Diaspora supported The Sect. Especially now that the Hollow Men were about.

Lok wished he could rebel and do something to end this madness. What The Sect was doing to various sentient races across the galaxy was no different then what Reptokk had done to his people after they had gone to war with the Lizard Colony back on Kaotika.

He had heard rumors of an underground movement called The Grand Militia, organized by someone Named Archon. The Militia was a guerrilla force opposed to The Sect's genocidal policies, and was made up of various races across hundreds of star systems. There were even rumors of Vampires joining up to end Sect rule. Lok hoped they would prevail.

But he did not know whom to speak to express his anti-Sect feelings. Even considering sedition against The

Sect meant a permanent trip to a mining colony, or, to be tortured to death. If he spoke to the wrong person he would be putting himself and his family at risk.

He sighed and checked the controls. He had nothing against *Blood*—it was a machine, incapable of emotion—only those who had perverted its use for evil. If only the humans of this era only knew what was transpiring on their planet. The Sect had taken all necessary precautions by infiltrating the appropriate positions in London Government and recruiting human collaborators looking for quick profit. So, unless a Grand Militia cell was in the vicinity, the humans of this reality were doomed.

It made him sick. He left the cab and sighed before heading to the dining car. The bartender there, a Vampire named Flick, smiled at him. His brown hair was slicked back against his skull and he was dressed in a white tuxedo shirt and black vest. A red bow-tie completed his uniform.

"Another long day, Lok?" he said. "What can I get you?"

"Kaotikan Black wine." Lok sighed. "Better make that two bottle, 8751 to be exact."

Flick poured him a glass. "You definitely know your vintage, my friend. The Sect must be paying you well."

Lok bypassed the glass and downed the bottle. Much to Flick's amusement. "My, my." Flick wagged his finger. "You're either very thirsty, or you have a lot on your mind, Lok."

"Perhaps I do, Flick." Lok wiped his mound against his sleeve. He nodded and Flick brought him the second bottle. He downed that as well and felt himself relax a bit. Yet his mind wandered back to his thoughts of insurrection; he had an idea.

"Flick, you've worked for The Sect for quite some time. How have they treated you?"

Flick eyed him over the rim of a large goblet he was polishing. He flashed his trademark smile, revealing his pointed vampire teeth. "No complaints…for now…but even if I did it wouldn't be safe to mention it, here."

Lok nodded. Flick was assuming a neutral viewpoint. Not putting himself in a dangerous position by making disdainful comments about his employer, but at the same time he wasn't endorsing them as well. Lok decided he'd try his luck. "What if you *did* have a problem with The Sect, Flick?"

Flick continued polishing his glasses. "Depends on who I was talking to?" He was playing it safe, soaking up what Lok had to say. Still, Lok's conscience urged him on.

Right before Lok gave his answer a Hollow Man entered the dining car and walked past the bar. Flick smiled at him. "Morning, Volz." The Hollow Man stopped and shot a vacuous look at Flick before continuing on to the next car. After Volz left Lok spoke: "What if I told you I was looking for a way out of my predicament?"

Flick studied Lok's eyes. Lok wished he had taken his telepathy classes seriously during his formative years in school. That way he could've read Flick's mind. He focused hard but could not pluck a single thought from the bartender's bartender's brain. "I'd say you were looking for trouble, Lok."

Lok nodded. He was already in too deep, any more pushing and he would expose his true intentions. Better to back off, he was still in the clear if he quit now.

"But I'd also say that you're quite brave for risking detection." Flick glanced around the dining car before leaning in closer. "Are you looking to make some sort of connection, Lok?"

Lok nodded. "As long as I knew I was in friendly territory. Perhaps."

Flick smiled again. He placed the glass down on the bar counter and rubbed his thumb across a green gemstone ring he wore on his forefinger. "Now we can have a friendly chat, with no interruptions."

*Flick is part of the underground!* "You're sure we're safe now?" Lok added.

"This ring has a dampening field embedded in it. We can talk for under a minute before I have to shut it off. Don't want the Hollow Men to think their detection devices are being screwed with. Now, Lok, what can I do for you."

Lok whispered: "Can you help me get out of this?"

"I can. But we would ask for something in return."

"I don't know." Lok looked around nervously. "I have a family to consider."

"Yet, you risked both yourself and them by talking to me."

Flick was right. Lok had risked much. And *now* was not the time to back out. "All right, Flick."

Flick grinned. "First, you'd need to transmit a destination report."

"To who?"

"A friend of mine."

"Militia man?"

"Shhhh," Flick said. "You trying to get us killed? What if I didn't have this ring?"

"I'll transmit it," Lok agreed. "Just tell me when and where."

"We'll talk some more, later," Flick said.

The door to the dining car opened again. This time four red-shirted Hollow Men barged in. The lead one approached Lok and Flick, Black Cube in hand. Lok remained cool and nursed his bottle, but Flick only smiled. "Welcome dear fellows. Beautiful day for a train ride."

"We detected a dampening field onboard the train," the Lead Hollow Man said. "We're conducting an extensive search for its origin."

Flick broke out an expensive bottle of French Champagne. He poured a glass. "In that case let us celebrate your dedication to duty."

※ 4 ※

With Robert still missing, and the Vampire woman nowhere to be found, Jack found himself spending more of his free time alone with the bottle.

He had never been a heavy-drinker, more of a social one, but the double blow of losing Robert and Mercedes' departure had been too much for his ego to bear. Add to that Scotland Yard's growing suspicions and Jack was fortunate to have remained sane.

Various suspects had already been summoned by Swanson for questioning, but ultimately none could be tied to the murders.

What Jack found odd was the way Seamus had disappeared. He had called on the Irishman's office more than three times in the past week and had no success.

Jack also found himself under continued surveillance. At first he did not notice, then one night, while out hunting the Vampire woman, he had spotted a man with a top hat following him from a distance. Just to be sure Jack had visited *The Sword & Lion* and sure enough after a few minutes he saw the same man sitting at a corner table, shadowing him. It appeared Swanson still considered him a prime suspect: and with the "Dear Boss" letter being signed "Jack the Ripper," how could he not?

All this contestation brought him back to his days as a young Army Lieutenant serving in South Africa in 1880. He had fought in the First Anglo-Boer war against the soldiers of the Transvaal, until he had been wounded at the battle of Bronkhorstspruit. Ultimately the Boers, no more than guerrilla fighters, had repulsed the mighty British Army. He thought harder. How could a group of Boers, mainly farmers, defeat the world's greatest empire?

Using reverse thinking would be the key to finding his quarry. Up until now he had thought like an Englishman, trying his best to utilize his lay of the city. But he needed to start thinking like a Vampire. And what did Vampires crave most?

Blood.

Checking the hospital would be a good start. But it might attract unwanted attention. Besides, this Vampire woman stalked her prey at night, and for some strange reason the women killed were prostitutes.

The key to finding her lay right under his nose, yet, he had ignored it until now. His heart raced in anticipation for nightfall to come so he could test his new strategy.

Jack put away his drink and brewed some coffee. After a long nap he felt refreshed and when the moon appeared in the night sky he got dressed and went outside, making sure he did not have a pursuer tracking him tonight.

He had a vampire to catch.

※5※

Mercedes sat on the balcony of her family's villa, overlooking the Iberian sea. The warm sun rays sparkled atop the surface of the water. Ships of commerce coming and going, like busy ants, from Barcelona's busy seaport.

"What are you thinking of, sister?" Mercedes' younger sister, Annabelle asked in Catalan, the indigenous language of the region.

Mercedes knew her sister meant well, but the question was illogical: how could she think of anything else other than Jack?

He had always been a strange man, attracted to things she could never quite follow, such as medical journals and chess—while she preferred the theater and equestrian activities. Perhaps being polar opposites had brought them together.

But she was under intense pressure from her family to return to London. Her coming here had already attracted enough attention from neighboring families, and her social circles were no doubt abuzz with gossip, attempting to pick apart her estrangement from Jack. Mercedes had to admit she was surprised by her own behavior.

She knew she couldn't stay here much longer, not because her family did not want her or were ashamed to house her after she'd left Jack, but they were staunch Catholics, and Mercedes, despite being raised in fairly liberal surroundings, was expected to be a loyal wife.

Living over nine hundred miles south of your husband was not the action of a devoted wife.

Two days later, after spending much time thinking about her future, she decided to buy passage back to London aboard a passenger liner headed for Southampton.

She had Annabelle and one of her attendants accompany her. Her younger sister had always wanted to visit England, and Mercedes needed the emotional support Annabelle would offer during the voyage home to London.

Little did Mercedes know that someone very dangerous had dispatched two Hollow Men to stalk her. Disguised as Spaniards they tracked her every move and when they learned of her impending journey to England they contacted their new mistress to request instruction.

So it was on the second day of the sea voyage that Mercedes' attendant was murdered in her cabin aboard the luxury liner *Ceylon*. Annabelle was spared, not out of Mercy, the Hollow Men were not known for that, but rather because they did not wish to wake Mercedes before they used a controlled anomaly to abduct her and bring her to Vampiress in London.

When Mercedes awoke she was cold. Her wrists hurt and when she looked up she saw they were bound tightly with rope, herself dangling in air like a slab of meat at a butcher's shop.

No wonder she was cold—she had been stripped bare. *No, this cannot be happening!* she thought. She closed her eyes again before re-opening them. Unfortunately it wasn't a dream.

Two shadows. No, three, approached her. She could hear the echoing of heels against the concrete floor. Only a dim, hazy light offered illumination in this dungeon. Her hands were numb, and she feared that her circulation would choke the life out of them.

Finally the three shadowy figures stopped just below her. She felt her body being lowered to the floor. Slowly the three figures came into view. The one in the middle: a woman with long black hair and pasty skin, high cheekbones, and a curved nose; she wore a crimson corset above leather breeches and thick boots.

"Comfortable?" she asked.

"Where are my traveling companions?" Mercedes asked.

"One is dead." Vampiress smiled. "But I spared your sister. Having lost a younger sibling myself, I know the pain."

"Where am I?"

Vampiress removed one of her leather gloves and back-handed Mercedes' jaw. She felt her neck snap backwards like a spring. For a few moments the room revolved around her; her three captors resembling a demonic carousel. "*We* ask the questions here, my dear. Remember that. I would hate to be forced into disfiguring that lovely face of yours. Why Jack would never forgive me. Which brings me to my next point. I'll need more information on your beloved husband, things that aren't already in our database."

Mercedes glanced at Vampiress in a vexatious manner. "You can't get—"

Vampiress slapped her again. This time across her other cheek, her body jerked backwards and she felt like her spine would crack.

"My dear you really must learn, restraint; be glad I am only hitting you at a fraction of my physical strength, otherwise, your head would've long been detached from your neck. Now, let us begin again… information on Jack."

Mercedes whispered incoherently. "Speak up dear," Vampiress chided. When the whispering continued, the Vampire woman leaned in closer to hear her words.

Mercedes spat blood in Vampiress' face. She wiped the stringy blood from her face. "I can tell you are going to be difficult." She raised her gloved hand again and struck Mercedes' chin.

―6―

"Don't get me wrong, Seamus, I'm grateful for you saving my life, but, I don't believe a word of it."

After the explosion Seamus had gone to investigate. He had found a severely injured Robert limping from the smoking ruins of the warehouse; Seamus was amazed at how someone could've survived such an ordeal. Not having the proper medical facilities available in 1888, he had been forced to blow his cover, and transport Robert to a secret medical facility on Atlas. From that point on, things had become complicated.

"It's all true, Robert," Seamus replied. "You can't tell me that this sort of technology exists in 1888 London? How else could I have transported you through time-space in a matter of seconds?" Around them various holographic screens listed Robert's vital signs. A robotic arm worked on the Englishman's shattered arm while he lay fastened to an operating table.

Robert knew the Irishman was right. But was Seamus truly an Irishman? Or posing as one. Robert was a trained detective; it was his nature to question things that did not seem right. He still had more questions to ask. "Where did you say we were?"

"Fifty miles beneath the surface of a planet named Atlas."

"Atlas?"

Seamus nodded. "A planet twenty light years from Earth. I work for its remaining inhabitants. I'm one of their Caretakers, assigned to monitor a chosen era for temporal transgressions."

Robert shook his head and rubbed his temples while the strange metallic arm buzzed about him like a incessant wasp.

"I know this is all a lot for you to take in mate. But I guarantee you I'm trying to protect Earth, not harm it. And now I need your help."

Robert tried to sit up but the restraints kept him in place. The metallic arm beeped at him while a floating sphere entered the room and scanned his body with a ray of red light. Robert cringed. "What the hell is that bloody thing?"

"Body-scanning probe." Seamus grinned. "It's checking your organs to make sure everything has healed properly; it's standard procedure around here."

"So you're not an alien, Seamus?"

Seamus rolled up his sleeve and whistled at the robotic arm. It stopped buzzing about Robert and extended itself toward the Irishman. "Mini-blood sample," he ordered it.

The claw of the arm transformed into a pinprick and drew a small amount of blood from Seamus' arm before depositing it into a small vial. "If that doesn't convince you, laddie, I don't know what will."

Robert couldn't hide his disappointment. A part of him wanted to believe this was a farce. But an unexplainable piece of technology had proven him otherwise. Still, he thirsted for more information. "It still doesn't explain how you became part of all this." Seamus grimaced and scratched his cheek.

"Now that, my friend is another tale."

"It appears we've got plenty of time, Seamus."

"Well, it all started while I was investigating a disappearance in St. Albans, Hertfordshire, near a rail station."

"Yes. I think Jack mentioned this to me. You were searching for a client's missing employee, right?"

Seamus nodded. "Yes, but what I left out of the story was what happened tome later in the investigation. After I had located the victim's body, drained of all blood, I heard a noise nearby. It sounded like an animal's snarl. Being the inquisitive soul I am, I proceeded to investigate further." Seamus paused for a moment and swallowed hard. No doubt he was reliving an episode from his life that he would rather forget. Robert understood Seamus' hesitation, but was eager to hear the rest of the tale.

"So…what happened?"

Seamus exhaled. "I walked a few steps, and to my right in an alley just under the stairway leading away from the platform I saw a shape hunched over another body. I pointed my revolver at it and ordered it to step out of the darkness. At first it stopped, then, before I could take another breath it was on me, my revolver had been knocked out of my hand and its gloved hands were around my throat, choking the life out of me. I was so busy trying to claw out of its grip that I only caught a glimpse of its face. It was a woman, beautiful, but her lips and fangs were stained with blood that dripped over my face. As hard as I tried I could not break free of her grip. She proceeded in choking me to death."

"You died?"

"Yes. But what happened afterwards was the strangest thing I ever saw. I awoke in a room, similar to this; just as you did. Standing over me was the face of an old man with a long wispy beard. He told me that his people (Atlasians) had brought me back to life. Of course, I thought he was lying; at first I called him 'St. Peter,' thinking I had already died and gone to heaven. Over the next few days this man, who called himself Archon, explained his purpose, and how he and the remaining population of his planet, Atlas, were tasked with preserving universal timelines. He asked me for his help, and told me I could work for him as one of his 'Caretakers.' Helping him combat The Sect."

Robert held up his hand. "The Sect?"

"Yes." Seamus ordered two cups of coffee from a terminal. "A ruthless Vampire organization bent on reclaiming their lost glory. They alter timelines, to benefit their agenda. The results often do not favor other sentient species." Another floating sphere entered the room. Its two metallic arms carried a small metal tray with two steaming cups of coffee. Robert drank it heartily; it was just what he needed.

"Naturally I felt indebted to Archon. He gave me my assignment: to track down and prevent Vampiress–the female vampire who had murdered me–from accomplishing her agenda. I didn't need any added incentive and gladly signed on as a caretaker. "

"I know of her," Robert said. "She interrogated me in the warehouse."

"She must be stopped," Seamus added. "But despite the technology at my disposal, I'll need help. And that is where you and Jack come in."

Robert finished his coffee. "I take it you have a plan?"

"Yes, but if we succeed, it will cost us our lives."

# SEVEN

THE FIRST WHORE JACK QUESTIONED nearly took his head off.

"I don't talk to coppers," she said, after he had ducked her punch. "So kindly fuck off."

"I'm no policeman," Jack replied, handing her a silver half crown. When the ruddy-faced woman saw Queen Victoria's face glimmering on the coin's surface her eyes lit up like a street urchin in front of a bakery window.

"Well in that case, love, I'm all ears. Or would you care to shag first?"

Jack tried containing a burst of laughter that threatened to explode from his lips. "Not today, but I *would* like some information."

The woman's eyes narrowed. "What type of information?"

"About the killings. Do you know anything about them?"

"I thought you said you weren't a bloody copper?" For a moment Jack thought she was going to take another swing at him.

"No…just a concerned citizen." He pressed another half-crown into her palm. "Please, this is very important."

"Very well." She pocketed the coin in her dress pocket. "All the girls are scared. They talk about a She-Demon stalking the street. Punishing them for their transgressions, since they're women of ill-repute."

Jack's hopes rose. This She-Demon had to be the Vampire woman he was looking for. "What else?"

"Me and two of the other girls were talking, they've got no other means to support themselves, that's the only reason they risk their lives on the streets at night." The woman paused and wiped away a stray tear from her cheek. "Same as me, love, I have two little ones to feed."

"Can you tell me anything more about this She-Demon?"

"Rumor is that she goes by the name of Vampiress. She poses as a man at first to lure her victims — don't ask me how she does it — then…kills whoever is unlucky enough to cross her path."

So now Jack had a name. *Maybe Seamus might know something about this Vampiress. But why was this Vampiress stalking women? And why in Whitechapel?*

"I've run across her path and know how vicious she can be. And thanks to you I know her name." Jack kissed the woman on the cheek and pressed a third coin in her grubby palm. She smelled like alcohol and tobacco all rolled up into one but he didn't mind. She giggled like a shy schoolgirl.

"Well if there's nothing else I'll be on my way." Before Jack turned to walk off, the woman–whom he learned went by the name of Oral Annie–placed her hand on Jack's arm.

"There is one more thing, love." Annie looked around to make sure no one was around them, and apart from a homeless man sleeping in an alleyway it was all clear. "I've got a friend, her name's Mickie, she might be able to tell you more about this Vampiress."

Jack was intrigued. "Really? How so?"

Annie leaned in closer. "Because, she's the only girl who's survived a Vampiress attack."

The address Annie gave Jack took him to a dingy apartment building in the heart of East London. The hallway to the apartment smelled musty and was devoid of light except for one dangling bulb that flickered like a firefly, making it difficult to read the apartment numbers on the doors. When he finally found the apartment he was looking for he knocked.

He waited for what seemed like forever before trying the door again. Finally it opened, a young boy, not much older than five years, stared up at him. He wore a dirty linen shirt and worn overalls over bare feet.

"Can I speak to Martha Carter?"

The boy wiped his runny nose. "She's with a customer now," the boy said. "You'll have to wait."

Jack's face turned red and he felt for the child, having to endure this type of environment at such a young age was unfortunate. A few moments later a beefy man wearing a derby and a tight-fitting suit appeared at the door. He avoided Jack's glare and made a hasty exit.

"You next?"

Jack turned his head and saw Martha Carter standing before him. She looked like she was in her mid-forties, but Jack had a feeling she was much younger than her outward appearance. "Annie sent me."

"Oral Annie? Well c'mon in, mate, don't stand in the hallway like a fifteen-year-old with the first-time jitters."

"I'm actually married," Jack said.

"Of course," Martha said, "most of my customers are." Jack took off his hat and entered the apartment. It was as unkempt as the building it occupied. Clothes lay strewn all over the living room floor, and it was sparsely decorated. "Take the gentleman's cloak, Nigel," she told the boy.

"I'm actually here to talk, and won't be staying long."

Martha looked confusedly at him. "Talk about what? If you wish to confess your sins there's a church down the street," she said coarsely.

"I'll pay you." Jack handed her a few shillings.

"Fine then, talk."

"Annie told me you survived an attack by someone called, Vampiress." At the mention of that name the blood drained from Martha's face, and for a moment she too looked like a vampire.

"Aye, but why would you want anything to do with her?" Martha unbuttoned the top of her blouse and showed Jack a milky scar across her throat. "That cheeky cunt did this to me. Was lucky to know a nurse nearby who patched me up before I fucking bled to death."

"Did you go to the police?"

"I sure did, but you don't think those wankers would believe the words of a common street whore. When I told them a bloody demon attacked me they bloody threatened to have me locked up if I didn't leave the station."

Jack nodded. "I know what you mean. Now this is important, Martha, can you tell me anything about Vampiress that you remember."

Martha started thinking; she walked over toward a dresser and removed a small circular object; she handed it to Jack. "I tore that off her corset before I took off. Lucky for me I had just gone shopping earlier that day and was carrying a bag of groceries. The bitch went crazy when she saw I had a clove of garlic in my groceries and I used it against her to escape."

Jack studied the object. It looked like a small medal. In the center was a logo similar to the one inscribed on the blade Vampiress had hurled at him: a bat hovering over a crest depicting two crossed swords. "One more thing, Vampiress spoke to me after she'd cut my throat. She said: 'even though I wasn't one of the five traitors, she'd enjoy me for a quick snack.' I don't know who these 'five traitors' are, or how that's gonna help you."

Jack didn't know either, but he felt hopeful. "Trust me Martha, you may have just helped save lives."

※ 2 ※

"Under my leadership, disloyalty will not be tolerated."

After they had arrived at Liverpool Street Station *Blood* had been boarded by Vampiress and four Hollow Men. Despite his disdain for the woman, Lok welcomed her onboard in a gracious manner befitting one of her rank and heritage. Now that he was in league with Flick he didn't want to raise any suspicion.

"Yes, mistress," Lok said. He felt like a lowly sycophant, but had to appeal to Vampiress' arrogance. Her aura was well-renowned throughout the Sect.

"You come here highly recommended, Conductor Lok. You served with distinction onboard the Viceroy's cruiser as an engineer?"

He nodded, and did his best to avoid extended eye contact with her. For some reason he felt she would pluck his seditious thoughts from his mind and have him executed on the spot.

"Yes, mistress," he repeated. He wished he was back onboard the cruiser, away from this genocidal place.

"Excellent. Let us proceed: to prevent any future insurrections, I have decided to make an example of one crew member…to be selected at random of course."

Lok's heart dropped into his stomach, and his blood froze in his veins. "Mistress, I do not understand, the previous crew has already been dealt with; everyone here is loyal to The Sect."

Vampiress turned toward him and smiled. "Of course they are, Conductor, I was referring to a clandestine source. You see, the Hollow Men recently intercepted a Grand Militia signal originating from *Blood*, some sort of dampening field used to mask conversations."

Lok composed himself. "Please mistress, I beg you. Do not kill one of our own, I'm sure the Hollow Men will locate the perpetrator."

"Perhaps," Vampiress said slyly, "but if you *know* who the perpetrator is Conductor Lok, then we can dispense with the random execution."

She had him in a difficult position. To admit he knew the perpetrator would expose him as well, and endanger Flick's cell. But if he remained silent, the safe move, an innocent would die.

Part of him wished he never spoke with Flick in the dining car.

"Well Conductor, I am waiting." Around him the whirlpools eyes of the Hollow Men swirled expectantly.

"I know of no such Vampire that could be disloyal."

"Then the execution shall commence immediately."

"Very well mistress, I shall be in my quarters."

Vampiress put a hand on his shoulder. It felt cold, even though it was gloved. "Ohh no, Conductor, you shall remain here to watch the execution, it shall take place here, inside the first car."

"But, I have important work to attend to," he lied.

"It can wait; surely you understand the importance of discipline." She turned toward the Hollow Men. "Bring the Stoker, Rolfe."

Lok wanted to yell at the top of his voice and tear Vampiress' eyes out with his nails, then, take those eyes, which have no doubt gazed upon countless executions, and ram them down the throats of these insidious Hollow Men.

Less than two minutes later Rolfe was brought before him. A red bruise on his left cheekbone, it healed quickly due to Rolfe's Vampire metabolism, but Lok knew the worst was yet to come. "Conductor why am I here?"

"Because you are a traitor, that's why," Vampiress said.

Rolfe ignored her words and looked at Lok. "Conductor, please, I've been cleared of any wrongdoing." Lok's heart cried out for him to act.

Vampiress slapped Rolfe across his right cheekbone. "You should be addressing me, worm. I am in command now." She nodded to the Hollow Men, who forced Rolfe to his knees. "I'm sorry, Rolfe," Lok said. If these were the types of sacrifices he had to make then he knew he would be damned.

One of the Hollow Men drew a Black Cube from inside his Jacket and activated it. It started pulsing before a white light shot out from it and engulfed Rolfe. He screamed in pain alongside Lok's conscience as the white energy extirpated his essence. His skin turned from a vampire white to a dull beige hue. Lok's fingers ached as he clenched and unclenched his fists.

After a few moments Rolfe collapsed face-first. The Hollow Men dragged his lifeless hulk out of the first car. Vampiress smiled at Lok, as if she had just done her good deed for the day. "Carry on, Conductor."

Lok would carry on, but whether or not his soul could was another matter.

"I watched a good vampire die today."

Lok had forced Flick to meet him inside the main lobby of the Great Western Royal Hotel, near Paddington station, away from the prying whirlpools of Hollow Men. The bartender kept looking around nervously. But despite his jittery exterior, his voice remained calm. "More innocents will die if we don't stay the course. I never said this was going to be easy, Conductor."

"I know, but you don't know how much I wanted to kill Vampiress today."

"If you had even attempted it, both you and I, and, the rest of the crew would've been killed, immediately. I know watching Rolfe die was difficult; you did the right thing, Lok."

Lok was not so sure about that. "I want the name of that London Grand Militia operative."

"I'm not sure that's such a good idea. The situation is already precarious, let's not unsteady it further."

"What do you mean?"

Flick leaned in closer. "We're planning a major operation."

"When?"

"Soon," Flick whispered. He stood up and put on his jacket. "Don't do anything rash, Conductor. Your conscience is the least of our problems. Wait for me to contact you. Or else we'll all end up like Rolfe."

-3-

When Jack got home from Martha's apartment he found Robert and Seamus waiting for him in his living room.

"Robert!" Jack hugged his brother and looked him up and down. "I had given you up for dead."

"I *was* dead, before Seamus had me resurrected." Jack did not know what his brother meant but he turned toward Seamus and shook the Irishman's hand.

"I've been looking for you too."

Seamus smiled. "I know, I'm sorry Jack, I've been busy."

"What about your ankle injury?"

Seamus looked at Jack abashedly. "Sorry to have deceived you Jack; it was an act, I was monitoring the warehouse and did not want to endanger you any further. I was hoping you'd lose interest once I backed out of our investigation; I see it hasn't."

"I don't understand; what warehouse?" Jack turned to Robert. "What's going on here?"

"You'll never believe where I've been Jack, it was bloody amazing."

Jack chuckled. "Try me."

They sat there talking. About Atlas, about Archon, about Vampiress, about the Grand Militia. Jack was not shocked in the least bit, after what he'd been through, this information was more relieving than confusing, at least now he could fill in the missing pieces.

"So what's next?" Jack asked.

"The Militia is planning an operation and we've got a Vampire on the inside that is working with us,"

Seamus said. "But we need help afterwards, to clean up the mess. You've got vampires and human collaborators in London that need to be arrested after we've dealt with Vampiress and her bunch."

Jack looked at Robert. "You think you can convince him?"

"Swanson?" Robert laughed. "He may not like me much but he respects my opinions. Yeah, I can sway the old man."

"While you were gone, Swanson came here and interrogated me, Robert, he now considers me a prime suspect in those prostitute murders."

"Yes but now we know Vampiress is killing those girls, I'll be your alibi."

"You think he'll believe us? Without any solid evidence?"

Robert patted Jack's shoulder. "Leave that to me."

Next morning Robert and Jack arrived at Scotland Yard. Everyone there stared at Robert as if he had risen from the dead; but afterwards greeted him and looked relieved that one of their own was safe. After explaining his absence story Swanson looked at Robert as if he had gone insane. "You go missing for over a week, show up out of nowhere, and expect me to believe this shit tale?"

"It's true, chief," Robert said confidently.

Swanson's mustache twitched sideways and he rubbed his eyes. "A mythical planet named Atlas?

Time-travelers? Vampires? You forgot to add the Loch Ness Monster in for good measure."

"And you!" Swanson pointed at Jack. "You were seen in Whitechapel last night. Didn't I warn you when I came to your house?"

"He's not the murderer," Robert interjected. "I can vouch for him."

"How can you?" Swanson said sarcastically. "Weren't you busy chasing Vampires in outer-space with your time-traveling Irishman?" He called out for two Police Constables, when they arrived Swanson pointed at Jack and ordered his arrest, they dragged Jack away, who, surprisingly did not resist. Robert tried stopping them from hauling Jack down to the detention cells, but two of his colleagues restrained him.

"I *swear*, Jack, I'll find a way to get you out of this mess!"

Jack did not look hopeful.

# Eight

Swanson ordered Robert to be released. The younger man scowled at both of his colleagues before turning on his supervisor. "You've just arrested an innocent man."

Swanson pondered Robert's words for a moment. "Perhaps, but we'll question him, and, if he is truly innocent, he'll be released."

"I tell you he's innocent!"

"Robert, you're an excellent detective," Swanson began, "but you're letting your personal feelings obscure your judgment. "Go home, relax for a few days, then come back to work, and we'll talk about your absence."

Robert felt as if he had just wasted the last hour of his life. "But I've already told you chief where I've been. Are you deaf?"

Swanson furrowed his bushy eyebrows. "Robert, I won't tell you again, go home, before I'm forced to lock you up as well."

※ 2 ※

Jack sat on a bench and studied his surroundings. It was a basic concrete prison cell, a pail stood in the corner while a ray of light filtered through the barred window, casting a white square on the charcoal floor.

He had faith in his innocence, and knew he would eventually be freed. The police had no firm evidence against him. But he was running out of time and he did not want to be sitting on the sidelines when Seamus' plan went into effect. "Bollocks!" he said angrily as he stood up and kicked air. It did not improve his situation but he felt better.

"Having trouble, Jack?"

Jack spun around. Floating before him was Seamus, his image outlined in white, giving the Irishman a celestial look. "Good God, Seamus, you're a blessed sight!"

"I leave you two alone for a few minutes and you get all locked up."

"Can you get me out?"

"Hmmm...I can try." Seamus' image disappeared and the room darkened.

"Seamus? Seamus!"

Seamus' image reappeared. "I'm back."

"Where'd you go?"

Seamus looked worried. "We've got problems Jack, I just learned why Vampiress is killing those women. But I'll need to get you out first. Stand back!"

Jack took two steps back. Seamus' image disappeared again before a doorway appeared out of nowhere. The Irishman's head popped through it and he waved Jack through. "C'mon man, hurry!"

"Is it safe?"

"Of course."

Jack walked through the portal. He felt light-headed at first but then his body grew accustomed to his new surroundings. "Took me awhile to get used to shifting as well. Keep in mind Jack, this technology, it's centuries ahead of our current development stage, it's natural for your body to experience side-effects at first."

Seconds later they were in front of the building where Seamus' office was located. "Beats taking a taxi, ehh Jack? No need to tip the driver." He said lightheartedly.

"You mentioned something about information why these women were being murdered by Vampiress?"

Seamus' demeanor turned serious. "Yes, I hacked into her computer and that's where I found the information."

"Hacked?"

"Yes, that means I used my computer to infiltrate hers." Jack nodded. "I see." But the truth was, he didn't completely. "Now, let me show you what I found." They left the street and walked toward Seamus' office.

※-3-※

The killing of the Stoker, Rolfe, weighed heavily on Vampiress' mind.

But it had to be done. She had to send a message that she was leader. She knew there were traitors amongst her. But until know they had evaded her. This was Ambrogio's fault. He had grown lax and allowed Grand Militia operatives to gain a foothold in this cell. She was happy to have killed him and rid The Sect of his incompetence.

Despite their expertise, it would take time to get the Hollow Men to locate the traitors, and the warehouse needed to be restored to a state where it could resume operations. That meant more corrupt humans in influential posts needed to be located and bribed in order to prevent detection.

And then there was Jack's fiancé, she too had a part to play in her plan; maybe she could use her as a pawn to rid the Sect of Jack's interference. She had a hunch he would lead her to the Grand Militia. Vampiress had to assume Jack was working as one of them.

So much to do, so little time. The bane of leadership, but she was determined to prove herself as a Section Chief to The Sect, and to her father. Her thoughts made her weary and she drifted off.

The days after Renault's death were the hardest for Fiolia. She had lost her best friend and her twin. It seemed as if a part of her had died. While she had been re-admitted to the academy she longed to return home on leave.

She had attempted to hang herself once from a tree in the woods behind her family's villa, and failed. Instead of snapping her neck the branch itself had snapped. So instead of falling to her death, she simply, fell.

The second time she had tried killing herself she had ingested poison in her room, but a house servant had found her shortly afterwards and had called for help. She had failed twice. *I cannot even kill myself*, she had once thought. *I'm a total failure.*

Her father would have none of her sulking and instead told her that she would accompany him on a mission.

"Where are we going?" she asked.

"Bring your weapons," was his answer.

Their family's personal guard escorted them. Fiolia had no idea where they were going, and every time she asked one of her father's guards she got no response.

They arrived in the city of Kant. A hotbed of moderate activity who had no love for The Sect. She knew there had been labor disputes here. Her father had revealed to her how the Viceroy had ordered him here to settle an issue with the Energy Guild, an organization that was vital to the survival of the First City's defenses.

The first Lord of Kant, a moderate vampire by the name of Xavier Nik, welcomed them and escorted them to the energy mines. There, the workers mined the precious ores that powered the First city's economy. "What is the current status of the energy guild's plans for strike?"

Nik sighed. "It is to commence in two days."

"Have you resumed negotiations?"

Nik shook his head to indicate that he hadn't.

"Take us to the energy guild's main office."

Nik looked surprised by this request. "For what purpose Lord Verchase?"

"I wish to question their President, and resolve the impending strike."

Nik smiled politely. "My dear Baron, that will not be necessary, I have already told you that the guild has rejected our offers. They plan to strike." Fiolia watched intently the events that were unfolding before her young eyes, her right hand clenched and unclenched the hilt of her sheathed dagger.

"No doubt because of your incompetence Lord Nik, by decree of the Viceroy, I am under orders to question the Guild President and come to a final resolution."

Lord Nik's polite demeanor disappeared. "I would like to see these orders!" When Verchase showed them to Nik, the First Lord's face descended into a pool of frustrated wrinkles.

"Now, take me to the office," Verchase ordered.

Guild President Smelt made them wait for almost an hour before admitting Nik and Verchase's entourage into his office. He was a corpulent man with a row of chins that descended down the front of his neck. Fiolia could tell by her father's solemn silence that he wasn't happy to have be kept waiting.

"Lord Nik, and Baron Verchase? To what do I owe the honor?" he said smugly. Fiolia looked at him disgustedly as his chins jiggled like pudding.

Nik was silent, but Baron Verchase wasted no time in speaking. "You are currently close to engaging in sedition by issuing this strike, President Smelt. I have arrived to put an end to it."

Smelt laughed heartily, and when he did Fiolia felt the office floor vibrate under her boots. "By whose authority? Yours?" Smelt stood up. He towered over both her father and Nik, but Baron Verchase did not look intimidated.

"By authority of the Viceroy," Verchase said calmly.

"The Viceroy has no right, it is written in Kant's deed that the Energy Guild has the right to enforce strikes when it deems inadequate working conditions:

the main shaft does not have proper ventilation, and my men haven't received new safety equipment which was promised two years ago. "

"The Viceroy has sixty-two other provinces which also have needs, you must be patient."

Smelt did not appear perturbed. "That is not my concern Baron Verchase."

Verchase turned toward his guards. "Go fetch me two miners, and be quick about it." Fiola had no idea what her father was up to, but she had a feeling Smelt would not benefit from it.

"What is this all about Nik?" Smelt said. "Why have you brought this," he turned toward Verchase, his meaty arms outstretched, "bureaucrat to my office?"

"This is not my doing, Smelt," Nik said subserviently. "I only brought him here." To Fiolia it felt as if Smelt ran Kant instead of Lord Nik.

The guards returned, with two disheveled miners in overalls. They looked at Smelt confusedly. Verchase turned toward the first miner, a man with one ear missing. *Probably the result of a mining accident and not enough funds to undergo surgical reconstruction,* Fiolia thought. "Who is the Vice President of the Guild?" Verchase asked him.

One-ear looked at Verchase before turning toward Smelt, then back again at Verchase. "We have none, my Lord, the office is currently…vacant."

"So you allowed President Smelt to approve the strike without appointing a Vice-President to confer with?"

The miner was speechless. Verchase turned toward the second miner, this one was shorter in stature than one-ear, and had protruding fangs. "What is your name?" Verchase asked fangs.

"Mortimer, m'lord." Verchase nodded before drawing his pulse gun. He fired a round into Smelt's knee, the limb disintegrated into nothingness. Smelt, minus one limb, lost his balance and crashed to the floor. The vibration caused Fiolia to nearly lose her balance as well. Everyone in the room was in shock, except Verchase and his personal guard. "Mortimer, as an official representative of the Viceroy's Imperial Office, I hereby appoint you Vice-President of the Energy Guild." Everyone in the room was speechless. Nik's forehead, a waterfall of perspiration.

Smelt lay on the ground, helpless, like a blue hare caught in a hunter's trap. Verchase turned toward one-ear, who was near tears. "What is your name?"

One-ear mumbled incoherently. "Speak up!" Verchase said.

"Felgor…m-m'l-lord."

Verchase turned to Fiolia. She felt her father's shadow loom over her, and suddenly he was not the man who had sired her, but a stranger whom she did not know. "Vampiress," he said, calling her by her Academy battle-name. "Draw your weapon."

"Father?"

"Now girl....do it!"

She drew her bow and nocked an arrow. Fiolia had a bad feeling she knew who the target was. She pointed it to the ground. "Father...I...I..."

Baron Verchase pointed his pistol at Fiolia's head. "You have your orders."

Fiolia could not believe what her father was doing, it was bad enough that the rights of these Vampires were being violated, even if the decree did come from the Viceroy, but now he was pointing a weapon...at *her*! She raised her bow and fired it into Smelt's throat, the arrow had a disintegrator tip, which killed him instantly.

Verchase nodded and turned to Felgor. "I hereby appoint you President of the Energy Guild; be sure to act in the best interests of your Viceroy so this unfortunate episode will not be repeated."

A part of Fiolia wondered what her father would have done if she had not killed Smelt. Would he have killed her? By killing Smelt she fortunately never had to find out. That was how she comforted herself, knowing she had completed an important task. But this was not like killing the Maratak, this was one of her people.

She had gone back to the academy a different person, and when she graduated the name "Vampiress" soon became one that everyone in Kaotika feared. She had killed countless enemies, all in the name of the Sect. But she always kept Smelt's death ingrained in her memory, as a reminder of that day in Kant.

When Vampiress awoke from her slumber, she knew exactly what needed to be done. She ordered two Hollow Men to bring Mercedes to her office.

-4-

Jack watched as Seamus' bookcase transformed itself into a strange looking device with various screens and flashing lights. "Compliments of my friends on Atlas, not their most advanced computer, but it's powerful enough to crack The Sect's network."

"One would think they'd give you an army to fight Vampiress and her kind." Seamus sat down into a small leather chair in front of the main console and started pressing random buttons. "That's not how Archon and his people work, Jack, they like to operate with as few operatives field as possible, that way, if anyone gets captured, the damage to the Militia is limited. The same goes for their technology, they can't risk having their most advanced works falling in the wrong hands."

Jack appeared satisfied by Seamus' explanation and sat next to him. "Now what was it you said you found?" Seamus' fingers danced across the device's console. Jack had no idea what this machine did, or how it operated, but it still fascinated him.

"Take a look at this, Jack." Seamus pointed to one of the screens, which to Jack looked like a small window with words on it. It resembled a glowing newspaper page. Seamus noticed how Jack was mesmerized by the technology so he read. "This is part of a mission log. The women who've been killed so far: Mary Ann Nichols, Annie Chapman, Elizabeth Stride, Catherine Eddowes, all were women that were earmarked to be taken over by Sect operatives."

Jack looked puzzled. "What do you mean by 'taken over,' Seamus?"

Seamus paused for a moment. "The Sect operatives sent here were clones—that means they're artificial life forms serving as human replicas—created to act as scouts and gather information before the Sect's main cell arrived to begin their mission. The clones were programmed to assume the identity of these women as cover, so they'd assimilate faster into late 19th-century England."

It felt strange to Jack how Seamus described their present in past tense. But these were bizarre times. "There's more, Jack, but you're not going to like this."

"I already don't like this." Jack wiped the perspiration off his forehead with a handkerchief.

"The Sect's mission here to is to extract energy from humans. Thus, draining them of life force the Sect needs to help resurrect their declining population. Life force is priceless to Vampires, even more than blood since they possess the technology to convert it into other forms of useful energy. The previous Conductor of the train, a Vampire agent working with us, tried to stop it. Unfortunately he failed. But we had inserted Flick as back-up; a precautionary measure."

"So he's your man on the inside?"

Seamus nodded. "He's going to assist us onboard *Blood*. I only hope that when I collect the stolen energy I can return it to their hosts."

Jack wouldn't have believed that possible if Robert hadn't told him about Atlas and its remarkable technologies. "Suppose we're successful, Seamus, what's to prevent the Sect from coming back to finish the job later."

"Time incursion is a tricky thing Jack, there are an infinite number of realities, and the Sect knows that if they try and return the Atlasians will be able to track them easily since multiple incursions in the same realities leave ripples in time which the Grand Militia tracks. That's why the Sect infiltrates countless realities and timelines to diversify their operations. They're a desperate people remember? Archon formed the Grand Militia to act as a service branch against these blood-suckers."

Jack was amazed at the magnitude of this war that stretched across time. Seamus had obviously been trained extensively by this Archon to have so much knowledge of advanced technologies and procedures. But these beings from Atlas, despite being human in nature, acted in an omnipotent manner by recruiting races native to affected timelines to help them fight the Sect. Jack marveled at the efficiency of these mysterious people, and envied Robert for being exposed to such advanced medicine, he would've given anything to take a look at the machines that had resurrected his brother from certain death. The pieces of the puzzle were slowly coming together, but still one thing did not make sense. "I wonder why these 'clones' as you call them would turn against the Sect and go rogue."

Seamus looked over the screen and shook his head. "Unfortunately I could not locate that vital piece of information, Jack. But we do have a lead that may be able to answer that question."

Jack's eyes lit up. "How?"

"The Sect sent five clones here to gather information. Four are dead, which leaves one, and I have her name and address on file, a Mary Jane Kelly of 13 Miller's Court."

# Nine

Miller's Court was quiet and misty.

Using the portal device Jack and Seamus shifted near the last known recorded residence of Mary Jane Kelly. This was Jack's second shift, and like the first time, he felt dizzy before the effects wore off. "A few more shifts Jack and you'll be a pro at traveling through portals," Seamus told him before drawing a hand-held device from his pocket, which to Jack resembled a small, thin piece of paper with a glowing surface.

"Did you locate her?"

Seamus nodded. "She's twenty meters ahead of us, on the sidewalk."

"Another piece of amazing technology, these Atlasians are geniuses."

They walked briskly, Jack grasping his saber's hilt while Seamus led them toward the final woman. "Are you picking up Vampiress?" Jack asked, he was anxious to get another crack at this woman, and drew his saber, the moonlight glinted off its blade.

"No, but I'm getting something different, two different types of signatures, they're definitely not Vampiress, Jack."

"Who are they?"

Seamus put away the paper-thin device and drew a strange-looking pistol.

Up ahead a female shape came into view, paying through thin layers of mist. The street lanterns glowed like hazy yellow candles upon the cobblestone street flanking the sidewalk. "There, I see her." Jack pointed his saber, he saw two tall men on the other side of the street cross and head toward the woman, who was wearing a linen dress and had a shawl draped over her shoulders.

"I don't like the look of this." Seamus said.

The men came into view; they wore black suits and wore sunglasses over their eyes. "Who wears sunglasses at night?" Jack said.

"I have a feeling we're going to find out," Seamus said. He drew the paper-thin device again. "Strange. I'm getting a null reading from those two men."

"Why so strange?"

"Because usually Sect machinery gives off that type of signature, not regular operatives."

Jack scowled. "Where is Vampiress?"

One of the two men broke off from the other and started walking in their direction before the other tailed the woman. "I don't like this," Seamus said.

"I'll take this one," Jack said. A glowing object appeared in the suit-man's hand. It pulsated like a small yellow star.

"Jack get down!"

A yellow stream of energy erupted from the object. Jack slashed his saber and it deflected the blast; the object erupted again and Jack had to hit the ground to avoid being struck. Seamus fired his pistol at the man, he evaporated into white energy like a star going nova.

Jack got up and ran toward the second man, who was struggling with the woman. Seamus fired his weapon again but the man threw the woman down on the sidewalk before deflecting the blast with its shielded hand.

"Shit!" Jack said. He charged the creature with his saber, the battle rush he Felt many years ago serving in the Boer War returned. But this time he wasn't facing Dutch settlers fighting for freedom, but an unearthly creature with unknown powers. The creature unleashed a spray of energy which Jack deflected with his blade. In the corner of his eye, Jack saw the woman, Mary Jane Kelly, he presumed, watching in horror as she lay sprawled on the sidewalk.

The creature threw a punch at him and he was able to get his fists up to deflect the blow. His bones rattled in his body as he absorbed the blow, it felt as if a locomotive had driven over his arms. The creature grabbed Jack by the lapels of his jacket and pulled him closer to its face. Under the lantern light Jack saw behind its sunglasses, whirlpools swirled like vortexes in sockets where eyes should have been. Jack saw the whirlpools grow larger and larger until he felt the energy draining from his body.

He gathered his remaining strength and head-butted the creature in the forehead twice before it released him; Jack's temples throbbed with pain as the night mist swirled around him. He saw the creature above him, it collected its composure and drew a glowing cube from its pocket. *That must be the weapon that fired on us earlier,* he thought. He tried to get to his feet but couldn't. A flash of light appeared above him and the creature snarled before disappearing. The darkness returned; just another misty night.

"Jack are you all right?" Seamus appeared and thrust smelling salt under his nose. His head jerked upright as he came to his senses.

"I'm fine," Jack said in between breaths, "check on the girl." But to Jack and Seamus' amazement the girl was already on her feet. She kneeled next to Jack and placed a hand on his arm.

A surge of energy pulsed through his body and soon he felt his full strength return. She picked up Jack's saber and handed it to him as both he and

Seamus looked at her with disbelief. "Who are you two?" she asked. "And why did you try and save me?"

"We're trying to stop Vampiress," Jack said. "She and the Sect are trying to destroy my people." He figured he could trust this woman."Seamus here is an caretaker operative of a planet named Atlas."

Mary Jane Kelly's eyes widened. "Atlas? It is said that they are the most advanced race in this galaxy. Well, if you are aligned with the Atlasians then your cause is just."

"We know you're a clone," Seamus added, "but what we don't understand is why you defied your programming, why did you abandon your mission."

The woman's eyes looked tired, he knew that look before, seen it in thousands of patients in hospitals he had worked at. "Let us talk in more secure surroundings." She led them off the streets and they disappeared into the night.

It was a modest dwelling, Jack thought. Kelly brought them two cups of tea and they sat down around her small kitchen table and waited to hear her story.

"The five of us were sent to this timeline to observe humanity and report back to Sect Command before they could establish their base. I was the last of a special mold that was created on Grydus II, a military research base 6 light years from Kaotika. The Sect's mission was very ambitious, but genocidal. Without any opposition, they would've drained this timeline dry." She paused for a moment and looked down at her hands abashedly. "I and the others were not told of this, but one night we intercepted a transmission and learned of their intentions. We were outraged, trained as both scouts and healers for damaged Hollow Men, it contradicted our programming to allow, anyone, even our enemies to be harmed, let alone exterminated, so we sought out women whose identities we could borrow. And, with their permission we merged."

"Merged?" Jack said.

"But why would these human women want to merge with alien lifeforms?" Seamus asked.

Kelly turned toward Seamus. "Because Mr. McCoy, they were all living destitute lives, working as women of ill-repute and suffering from various sexually transmitted diseases. They were happy to accept our offer. But of course the Sect would never allow this so they assigned a ruthless Section Chief named Ambrogio to hunt us down, using Vampiress and Hollow Men troops." Kelly pointed at Jack's saber. "You're lucky to have such a weapon, Mr. Mansfield, Silver is the only metal that can deflect firepower from a Black Cube—the weapon of choice for Hollow Men."

"Vampiress tracked us down and murdered each of us, gaining strength in the process by violating our bodies and sucking our enhanced blood." She stopped and took a deep breath. "Your efforts are admirable, but stopping two Hollow Men will not be enough, she'll send more."

"We're planning a major assault on their locomotive, *Blood*," Seamus said. "Once the cell has been shut down, The Sect can no longer bother you."

Kelly looked grateful. "Then I wish the both of you Godspeed on your mission, and hope, will all my heart, you can stop the killing."

※ 2 ※

They left the house full of hope, yet knowing the challenge they faced would test their resolves. Both men were quiet, they walked home to clear their minds and decided to forgo shifting for another trip.

"What's on your mind Jack?"

Jack lit a cigarette, and exhaled, the smoke swirled around his face before dispersing. "Just trying to get myself mentally prepared. Truth is, I may never see Mercedes or Robert again."

Seamus nodded. "I face that question almost every day, it's hard, keeping my secret life as Caretaker for Atlas secret from my wife and children. It eats me up every time that I have to lie to them about it. And, that I may never return from any given mission, knowing that every action I take will never be known to them."

Jack finished his cigarette and tossed it down the slit of a sewage drain. "Then I guess I shouldn't be complaining, you're in this a lot deeper than me."

A light appeared before them and they stopped walking. To Jack it looked like a door opening into a dark room, the light eventually formed into the familiar face of a woman. Jack's eyes widened and he felt his heart drop into his stomach.

"Mercedes?"

She had a small bruise above her upper lip but apart from that seemed uninjured. Something sharp was pressed against her temple. It looked like an arrow head. "What's going on here?" Jack said angrily. "Where are you?"

"Jack…please…you have to come for me…" Her face disappeared and was replaced by….Vampiress! Her chalk face and dark eyes, foreboding and alluring, were filled with malice.

"Hello Jack, so we meet again."

Jack drew his saber and waved it at the Vampire woman's image. "What have you done with my wife, you vampire bitch?"

Vampiress laughed. "Mind your manners, or else I might be tempted to hurt her, you wouldn't want that…now would you, Jack?"

"What do you want Vampiress?" Seamus asked.

Her face turned toward Seamus. "Ahh, the great Seamus McCoy, my favorite Grand Militia operative.

I knew you'd want to get to the point." She laughed again. "I have Mercedes, and if you ever wish to see her alive again you will come to Liverpool Street station, and gentlemen, try not to be late."

The image disappeared, leaving Jack fuming in its wake. "When I find that filthy bloodsucking bitch, I'll kill her…I'll…"

"Calm yourself, Jack, don't you see? That's what she wants, for us to go in there all cocked and careless, we must remain calm."

Jack wiped a tear from his eye. "It's not your wife they're holding, Seamus."

"I know," the Irishman said compassionately, "but we need to be patient, and have a set plan before confronting her, or else we'll lose for sure."

Jack spent a minute trying to compose himself. He nodded and exhaled. "I know, Seamus, but I'll never forgive myself if Vampiress kills Mercedes."

※ 3 ※

They found Robert in Jack's home, sipping brandy and looking sullen. Jack stomped into the living room and unloaded his sabers onto the ground. When Robert saw his brother his eyes were alight. He rushed toward Jack. "Jack? My dear Lord, you've escaped!" Jack didn't know if his brother was more elated or surprised to see him.

"Robert, they've got Mercedes."

Robert looked at his brother alarmingly. "Who… the vampires?"

"Yes, somehow they must've tracked her down," Seamus added.

"But she's in Barcelona, with her family," Jack said.

"You mean she *was* in Barcelona, Jack. Somehow Vampiress must've tracked her down and plucked her from Spain. It's not uncommon, given The Sect uses controlled anomalies to travel through time and space—it's similar to shifting. That's how they're likely transporting the life force they've been stealing, and using a modified locomotive from this time period to look less conspicuous."

Seamus turned to Robert. "Any chance your boss Swanson can loan us some extra men?"

Robert shook his head. "He won't go for it, and now that Jack's escaped Swanson will probably think I helped him break out of prison, he's not aware of the technology you possess, Seamus."

"Well in that case you'll have to convince him Robert, we're going to need Scotland Yard to help clean up the mess we're about to make."

Robert finished his drink. "I don't like the sound of this Seamus."

"We've got to all be on one page, men, if we're to save Mercedes and rid this reality of the Sect incursion," the Irishman said, "I'm going to contact Flick and tell him to expect us; then, we'll draw up a plan before taking on The Sect. Our assault commences before dawn. "

Robert grabbed his gun and jacket before pouring everyone a round of brandy. Jack took a gulp and the warm liquor felt good as it eased into his stomach. "All right, Seamus, what's the plan?"

# Ten

Liverpool Street station loomed ahead of them, a structure filled with unknown portents.

Robert took the Atlasian weapon Seamus had given him and replaced it with his own weapon. Jack admired the trust Seamus had for Robert, the fact the three of them stood against staggering odds seemed admirable.

"I wish this could've been easier," Jack said, gripping his two sabers.

"Nothing worthwhile is ever easy, Jack."

Robert drew his Atlasian pistol. "Whatever happens gents, it was an honor knowing both of you."

"Listen, mate," Jack said, "we haven't lost yet."

"That's right," Seamus interjected, "but just in case we do fail, I've left a message beacon behind to instruct Atlas to send an operative to permanently shut down that warehouse harvesting those innocent citizens."

Seamus checked his pocket watch. "The departure time is in less than ten minutes, let's get inside the station and on that train."

They moved quietly and fast through the darkness. Around him Jack studied the peaceful London streets and the dark silhouettes of buildings clustered around Liverpool street station for any Sect activity. If things went according to plan he would rescue his wife and defeat the callous plans of Vampiress and the Sect.

They entered Liverpool street station from the main concourse. Activity was non-existent except for one janitor cleaning the floors. Jack looked around and studied his surroundings like an owl searching for prey.

Nothing. This seemed too easy, but he had a feeling the Sect would make their appearance in due time. They searched each platform until Seamus found the one where Lok's locomotive was located. *Blood*. It was a huge menacing hulk of steel, rods, wheels, pumps, and dome. Painted black and red, a large bat logo, wings outstretched, displayed proudly on its smoke box door. Knowing its true purpose was to facilitate genocide made Jack want it destroyed even more.

"Let's not waste any time standing around, Flick should be on board, waiting for us," Seamus said. As they neared *Blood* Jack could see strange cranes loading canisters into one of the boxcars. Jack found it strange there were no sentries or Sect personnel around to supervise the transaction. His heart beat even harder the closer they got to *Blood*.

"Say there my good chaps, would any of you have a light?"

Jack, Seamus and Robert all whirled around and saw an old man in a top hat and long coat emerge from behind one of the platform columns. He had a cigarette in his gloved hand and wiggled it at them as he slowly made his approach.

Seamus stepped forward. "I say old bloke, we're on business here, you must clear out."

The old man stopped and smiled. There was something in the smile that Jack did not trust. It was as unfathomable as a fox protecting a chicken coop.

"What makes you think I don't belong here, Irishman?" the old man said. He let out a burst of malefic laughter before his eyes transformed into whirlpools. Energy rays exploded from them just as Seamus deflected the blast with some sort of energy shield. "Hollow Men!" he yelled before he returned fire. The old man ducked to avoid being disintegrated and shed his disguise, revealing the black-suited antipathy of its true form.

The Hollow Man continued spewing energy from its eyes, but Seamus' shield held it in check. Robert trained his new weapon on the Hollow Man and vaporized it. "Let's get on the train," Seamus said. They ran toward *Blood*, as they did they watched the cranes finish their tasks and seal the boxcar doors.

Jack hoped Flick was waiting for them inside Blood, ready to help. But he snapped out of his thoughts when more Hollow Men—these wearing white shirts instead of red—appeared around them, materializing out of nowhere and firing strange-looking rifles at them. Jack deflected two rifle blasts with the silver saber blades and decapitated one Hollow Man before he noticed *Blood* slowly pulling out of the station. The smokestack began expelling billowy smoke before a shrill whistle sounded its message that Blood was on its way to its next destination, wherever that was. Another rank of Hollow Men flooded the platform, and Jack worried that they wouldn't be able to board *Blood*; the thought of losing Mercedes tortured his conscience. Seamus and Robert fired indiscriminately, vaporizing their opponents, while Seamus' shield took a pounding from enemy ordnance.

More and more Hollow Men appeared and for a moment Jack thought they would overrun them. Instead they began withdrawing, leaving an open corridor for the three men to approach the departing *Blood*.

"Seamus, this doesn't make sense," Jack said, as Robert kept up with them.

"Doesn't matter, Jack, we'll have to play along with whatever Vampiress has planned…and hope for the best, mate."

One of the boxcar doors opened, almost too conveniently for Jack's taste. "That's Flick," Seamus said, "he's unsealed one of the doors, giving us our chance to board."

The three men took turns leaping toward the boxcar's rail ladder before hauling themselves into the boxcar. As soon as the last of them were safely inside, the door automatically closed behind them, sealing them inside.

※-2-※

Inside the boxcar it was cold. Despite having Seamus and Robert with him, Jack felt alone.

"Won't Flick's actions be monitored by Sect security?" Robert asked Seamus. "He's risking a lot by helping us."

"He's got help, the Master Conductor, a vamp called Lok, is monitoring Sect activity onboard so Flick can aid us."

"Seamus, you're one resourceful bloke."

Seamus illuminated a small light that chased away the darkness surrounding them. "Where's Mercedes?" Jack asked.

"Three cars over, I'm also detecting null life signs again; more Hollow Men. and this time they're not even bothering to cloak themselves."

"Why should they?" Robert looked resolute. "They know we have to come to them."

"Then let's not keep the bastards waiting."

Seamus put a restraining hand on Jack's arm. "We can't just go blasting into the next car, it would be suicide."

"If you have a better idea Seamus, now's the time to hear it."

Seamus pulled out another small device. "As a matter of fact gents, I do."

Inside the supply car Vampiress waited for the enemy to come to her. She had kept Jack's fiancée, the Spanish woman, on a tight leash, literally. She figured seeing his wife with a collar would dishearten him. Good. She wanted it that way, she would use any advantage she could muster. After she had rid this reality of Jack and the Irishman Seamus McCoy, she would have dealt the Gran Militia a crippling defeat, something they had yet to taste during their struggle with her people. *Good*, Vampiress thought, *the first defeat is always the most painful. Maybe it will even tip the war's momentum in our favor.*

She slung her bow over her armored corset, the one with the Sect's bat crest inscribed on her bosom. "Come, my pretty," she told Mercedes, "we're off to see your beloved husband, soon, you two will be reunited."

The Spanish woman looked at her disconsolately. She had been forced to wear a prisoner's smock. Vampiress jerked the cord that was attached to Mercedes' collar and giggled. "What's wrong, my beauty? You should be happy, Jack is coming for you."

Mercedes cocked her head and spat in Vampiress' face. Volz and the other Hollow Men observed the exchange indifferently. Vampiress wiped the saliva from her face and jerked Mercedes' so hard that the Spanish woman lost her balance and landed on the floor. "There, I think I like you better down on the floor."

"Vampiress," Volz said. "Intruders."

Vampiress donned her battle helm, its comb decorated with the Sect's Bat crest. She drew her disruptor and awaited combat, gripping Mercedes' leash in her other hand.

The door at the end of the car blew open and smoke poured into the room. The car shook around her. Volz and his three Hollow Men searched for opponents to target but there were none. Then two humans appeared. Vampiress recognized them as McCoy and Robert, Jack's brother. But Jack was not with them. They fired their weapons at the Hollow Men who reciprocated with salvos from their black cubes.

Seconds later the two men made a suicidal charge at the Hollow Men.

"Kill them," Vampiress screamed. Seconds later the two humans lay dead at her feet. Mercedes hobbled over toward where Robert's body lay and broke into tears.

"Wait." Vampiress fired her disruptor at Seamus' body and the beam passed through it and tore a hole in the floor of the car. She gritted her teeth and hissed. "These aren't real…they're holograms!"

One of the reasons Jack liked Seamus was the Irishman had a penchant for ingenuity. Despite her vast resources and firepower, Vampiress' arrogance had been her undoing, and Seamus had ruthlessly exposed it when he sent the two holograms storming into the car.

By the time Vampiress and the Hollow Men figured out they'd been shammed, Robert and Seamus had shifted into the car and vaporized all Hollow Men, except for their leader, Volz: realizing he'd been defeated he dropped his black cube and surrendered. "That shifting trick was impressive," Robert said.

Jack charged Vampiress and sliced the disruptor's muzzle off with his reinforced silver-bladed saber, before spinning around and kicking the weapon out of her hand. She grabbed the leash, and jerked Mercedes toward her. Jack, seeing his wife restrained like a common house pet, prepared to slash another cut at Vampiress before she drew a knife and pressed it against Mercedes throat.

"Now, now Jack," she said haughtily, "you wouldn't want me to slice up this pretty face, would you?"

Mercedes struggled but Vampiress' superior vampire grip was too strong to break. "Kill her Jack! Save yourself," Mercedes cried.

"How romantic." Vampiress muttered a command in her native language and disappeared, taking Mercedes with her.

※-3-※

"Bloody hell," Jack said. Had he and the others come so close to victory, only to let that vampire bitch get the best of them at the end?

"I'm tracking her," Seamus said, eyeing his handheld device. "Found her! Let's go." Robert stayed behind to secure the Hollow Men's leader, whose name was Volz.

"Good, Let's end this, now."

Vampiress dragged Mercedes behind her as she made her way toward the cab. She hadn't lost yet, not if she could get to the Conductor first.

"Stop!"

Vampiress turned around. One of her own people had a disruptor trained on her. "You've lost Vampiress; release the girl and stand down."

"You!" She recognized the bartender, Flick. "Traitorous scum, collaborating with humans. I'll execute you myself."

"Going to be hard to do with me pointing this weapon at you…isn't it?"

Vampiress was fast, and before Flick could fire his disruptor at her she grabbed Mercedes and pushed her into him. Flick, not wanting to risk hitting Mercedes with weapon fire caught her, dropping his weapon, but he lost his footing and she fell on top of him.

When Flick got to his feet he had Mercedes in his hands. But Vampiress was gone. So was his disruptor.

Lok's eyes widened when Vampiress entered the cab pointing a weapon at him.

"Mistress? What is the meaning of this?"

"Are we approaching the anomaly portal?"

Lok nodded.

"Good. Rig the engine to detonate."

"What? Have you gone mad, woman?"

She felt like vaporizing him on the spot, but she did not wish to set off the alarm. Ordnance fire in the cab could alert the train's computer to shut down. It was a security precaution to prevent hijackings.

She smashed the hilt of the disruptor into Lok's forehead. The Conductor's skull was thick so she repeated the action until he lost consciousness and slumped to the ground before he rolled down the stairwell.

Smiling, she began programming the reactor to implode.

Jack's reunion with Mercedes was short-lived. They kissed and embraced like two lovebirds kept apart in separate cages.

"Are you all right, Flick?" Seamus asked.

"Yes," Flick said. He looked ashamed he couldn't stop Vampiress. "But she got my weapon."

"Where is she now?"

Flick pointed toward the front of the car. "She looked like she was headed to the main cab before she teleported out. I alerted Lok, but he isn't responding to my message."

"Shit." Seamus turned to Jack. "C'mon mate, we've got to get to her."

Jack kissed Mercedes again. "I'll come back to you, love. I promise." Mercedes tried to look hopeful, but when Seamus and Jack shifted out of the car she burst into tears.

*Almost done*, Vampiress thought. *A few more adjustments and I'll be done. If I can't win I'll destroy my enemies.*

"That's enough!"

Vampiress whirled around with her disruptor but Seamus was quick and stunned her with his pistol. She lost her balance and slithered toward the floor, but not before grasping the console and pressing one last command control. "You've failed, Irishman, you and your English lapdog will rue the day you crossed my path."

"What's she done, Seamus?" Jack asked.

The Irishman's eyes darted over the console before his facial features assumed a glum expression. "Not good. She's programmed the train's reactor to explode once it comes in contact with the anomaly."

"But it can be stopped, right?" Seamus handed the disruptor to Jack who kept it trained on the stunned Vampiress.

"I can, but not in time."

"I can help you."

Jack saw another Vampires appear, wearing overalls, he stepped out of the stairwell adjacent to the main reactor and ambled over toward the main command console. He was rubbing his head and looked slightly tousled. "I take it you're the Conductor?" Seamus said.

"Yes, Master Conductor Lok." He rubbed his temples before opening the outer door to the reactor. "I can deactivate the implosion sequence, but keep that cursed woman away from me while I work." He pointed at Vampiress, who looked like a rabid dog ready to bite someone. Lok uttered a few verbal codes into a command console inside the outer reactor door. The implosion countdown sequence stopped. Vampiress felt her muscles slowly returning to full strength. Even though she was hit with stun at point blank range her armor had absorbed the blast; she wasn't finished yet, no, she would wait for an opportune time to strike back at her enemies.

"There," Lok said, relieved. "It's done."

Jack was glad things had ended without catastrophe. Unfortunately his optimism was premature.

Vampiress charged Lok. "NOOOOOOOOOO!" She pushed Lok into the wall of the outer reactor door, causing it to open and knocking the conductor to the floor. A glowing red light flooded the compartment before Jack picked up the disruptor and trained it on Vampiress, who was trying to reprogram the train to explode.

Lok looked at Jack like he'd gone mad. "Don't fire that weapon! The reactor door is still open, and we're too close to the anomaly!" But his words came too late. Jack fired at Vampiress and she and Lok disappeared as a flash of light absorbed their bodies. Jack felt Blood shake around him and he lost his balance, he found himself inside the threshold between the outer reactor door and the main reactor, seconds later he saw a flash of red light around him and felt his body dissolving around him. He saw Vampiress and Lok, spinning around him in an alien dimension comprised of red and white light. Lok had his hands around Vampiress' wrists, and her hands were around his throat.

Jack's head was spinning. The dimension began contracting around him until he became enshrouded. He lost consciousness.

―4―

With Flick's help Seamus was able to stop *Blood* before it passed through the anomaly. But what of

Jack? Where had he gone? It seemed unfair that the Englishman had fought so hard against a determined enemy, only to be killed during the final struggle. But Flick was able to shed light on the dilemma, even if it was only a theory. "I'm no trans-dimensional physicist, but I once watched a broadcast via news feed that accidents like this used to happen during the early days of plasma reactors: any type of unstable elements that came into contact with unsecured reactor rooms sometimes caused time-displacements. Being so close to a controlled anomaly probably didn't help either. But in a way it's good that the accident happened on a planetary controlled anomaly and not on a space vessel near a the Sect-controlled inter-planetary portal. Then, tracking them would take forever since it was in outer space."

"So you mean to tell me Jack's still alive?" Robert asked.

"It's possible, in Earth's past, or future. The same goes for poor Lok and that nasty Vampiress." Seamus noticed that this possibility did not console Mercedes, who looked even more dejected than before. "After we've impounded *Blood* on Atlas, we'll go searching for Jack, my lady." He placed a reassuring hand on Mercedes' arm.

"I would like to come too," Robert added. "He is after all my blood."

Seamus shook his head. "I need you here, Robert, remember? To convince Swanson to arrest the corrupt human collaborators that were on Sect payroll. I'll give you access to evidence I've compiled over the past few months, that should help convince your pig-headed boss."

Robert nodded. "And clear my brother's name as well." Seamus looked out of the cab's window into the dark field of space where an infinite number of stars blinked back at him. "I wonder where Jack is, and how he's faring?"

# Epilogue

When he awoke he was lying in a meadow under a blue sky filled with a caravan of clouds.

His head throbbed as if someone had hit him with a cricket bat. Had he been drinking? If so where? He rolled around on the ground, a soft patch of green sod. A few paces from where he lay he saw his hat, around him his cloak was twisted around his body like thick coils of rope.

He was alone. But he did not feel alone. Inside his head he heard two other voices: The first voice, calling itself Vampiress, was begging him for blood, the other, a calm voice called Lok, was speaking to Vampiress, telling it to repent for its crimes. He tried to recall how these voices got into his head. Was he hallucinating? Or mad? Perhaps both. He wished he knew his name.

He looked around at his surroundings again. Where was he? How had he arrived here? Images of a beautiful Hispanic woman floated through his mind. She looked familiar. *Who was she?* He could not place her name. *Damn.*

More faces flooded his mind, and just when he felt as if he would recognize them, they became foreign again.

Around his waist were two sheathed swords. Am *I a soldier? No. You're a doctor,* said a voice. Was that his voice or one of the other two in the background.

*"You're a good doctor," said the voice of Vampiress. "And you must help your patient; you must find me blood."*

*"No, Jack! You mustn't."* This came from the other voice, the one called Lok.

So his name was Jack. That's a good start. But which voice should he listen to? Perhaps neither. He decided he would explore his new world to try and get answers. Taking his hat, he started walking, and pushed both Vampiress and Lok out of his thoughts.

He walked through the meadow until he came upon a strange-looking road. Adjacent to it was a large structure that looked like a stone cube, inscribed upon its surface was strange writing. He thought he had seen it once before. He would learn who he was, and what he was doing here, wherever here was.

In the distance he saw a group of men approaching. They marched together, in an orderly rank. The one leading the front of the column carried a long staff. As they got closer he noticed a large birdlike ornament made of gold mounted on the staff, beneath it hung a red banner with gold letters sewn upon it which spelled: SPQR. Again, his disjointed memory felt it had seen this emblem before. *But where?*

The column of men drew closer, and Jack could see them more clearly. The Man carrying the staff wore an animal pelt over his head which was tied under his neck. The others wore helms and strange armor and carried rectangular shields that were almost as tall as they were. Jack's fractured memory strained itself trying to recall where it had seen these types of soldiers before.

Behind the column was another group of men, but they were mounted on horses and wore shiny helms with red plumes. Perhaps they were the officers?

*"Jack, kill them!" said Vampiress. "They look dangerous." Almost immediately Lok chimed in. "Jack, find a place to hide, and study them first before making any aggressive moves."* The pain in his temples returned in spades and he buried his face in his palms and grunted.

When he lifted his face from his fingers, he was surrounded by the soldiers, they stared at him acrimoniously.

One of the three officers approached on horseback and spoke to Jack. He gesticulated as he spoke, trying to communicate with Jack. *"Defend yourself, Jack, or you'll be dead!" said Vampiress.*

*"If you won't go and hide then relax, and stand still,"* said Lok. *"Look non-threatening."*

One of the soldiers began inching his way toward Jack while the mounted officer with the red-plumed helmet kept talking to Jack—his voice louder now.

*"Jack don't do it," Lok begged.*

Jack drew his sword, and its blade shone pristinely under the sunlight. The soldiers began chattering excitedly amongst themselves. The officer on horseback spoke to them but Jack still didn't know what that mean. Was he ordering them to attack?

Jack plunged his sword into the exposed neck of the closest soldier and blood spurted onto the mortar road. He didn't stop there. With surprising agility he cut down four more soldiers before any of them could so much as take a jab at him with their spears and swords. Jack leaped into the air and took off the head of the mounted officer, the red-plumed helm with his head sailed through the sky before landing onto the meadow grass. He battled the remaining soldiers with a ferocity of a rabid creature. He did not know where he had got this strength but he was glad to possess it. He ripped off limbs and used them to beat down his opponents. Jack felt like an unstoppable cyclone: leaving blood, gristle and dented armor in his wake.

When the soldiers lay dead at his feet he was surprised to still feel energetic. He looked upon the carnage he had inflicted and smiled, but, moments later, he scowled and cursed himself for being rash. *What did I do? Why did I act like an animal?*

"*Because you're a Bloody Ripper,*" Vampiress said.

Jack dropped his sword and dropped to his knees, burying his face in his blood-stained palms, while inside his brain Vampiress and Lok fought a relentless battle for control of his thoughts.

He felt something warm pool around his knees. When he looked up he saw his reflection in a puddle of glistening blood. He did not know what to do next, but he would think of something.

**The Bloody Ripper will return in**
***The Leopard Stratagem*, coming Summer 2014**

# Final Thoughts

*The Bloody Ripper* is the second book in a planned trilogy of prequel novels that can be read separately as standalones, or as a growing part of the Leopard King Universe. You may wish to start with my debut novel, *The Leopard Vanguard*, the first part of the Leopard King Saga, which tells the story of Tullus and Celestra the Incantra Leopardess. But you do not have to read *The Leopard Vanguard* to understand, or enjoy, *The Bloody Ripper* or any of the other two books that comprise the trilogy. The versatility of *The Bloody Ripper*, much like its predecessor, *Kill Zombies*, and the final standalone that will follow, is they set the stage for three key antagonists that will appear in the second part of the Leopard King Saga: *The Leopard Stratagem*, to be released in summer 2014. Now we move to the final book in the prequel trilogy. To the Kingdom of Rek, where a blind shepherd boy is about to make a startling discovery…

## ❖Also by T.A. Uner❖

The Leopard Vanguard:
Tome One of the Leopard King Saga

Kill Zombies

Stone Ram (*Coming Soon*)

Printed in Great Britain
by Amazon.co.uk, Ltd.,
Marston Gate.